The Edge of Madness

Raymond Gaynor

Aignos Publishing
an imprint of Savant Books and
Publications Honolulu, HI, USA
2020

Published in the USA by Aignos Publishing LLC
an imprint of Savant Books and Publications LLC
2630 Kapiolani Blvd #1601
Honolulu, HI 96826
http://www.savantbooksandpublications.com

Printed in the USA

Edited by Michael Davis
Cover by Daniel S. Janik
Cover image ID 31788291 © Dmytro Tolokonov
Dreamstime.com

13-digit ISBN: 978-0-9996938-5-8

First Edition: June 2020
Library of Congress Control Number: 2020939777

Dedication

To Draff Rob Brie [Septican-Smite], Simi Andry Jan [Jan-Rho], Billie Frann Frunk [Tordon-Cass], their parents, children, heirs and assigns.

Acknowledgements

I will always be indebted to William Maltese, my dear friend, colleague, mentor and co-author of TOTAL MELTDOWN (Borgo/Wildside), the prequel to this work that set the stage for this entirely new look at a seemingly crazy, out-of-control world.

Chapter 1

Although he wouldn't completely understand it until much later, it began well before he was born a pudgy-looking, seven and a half pound naked ball of flesh, fat, gristle and bone, screaming its head off. And why shouldn't he have protested? Every trusted thing he'd known had been ripped from him: the constant warmth; the gentle, protective floating feeling; the ruddy aura that had always surrounded and protected him, the ever-present thump-hiss, thump-hiss, thump-hiss in the background that, like a metronome, established the meter of his universe. Even the occasional, distant, often perplexing background sounds, a kind of symphony inexplicably directed at him by some higher, beneficent power whose sole reason for being was to watch over and protect him. Moments ago he was as he knew and imagined himself: the center of all that was, is, and would ever be. Now he was...he really didn't have a clue, except that every second he was fighting for his life.

Before that fateful moment, he'd lived happily enough in

his closed, familiar world in which fingers and toes slithered constantly in and through a wet, warm, slippery ocean that surrounded and permeated him. Even the discovery of the tough, protective wall at arm's length away in every direction (it had apparently always been there though it had completely eluded him until recently)—the limiting edge of the carefully enclosed world he'd slowly discovered and explored—hadn't daunted him. Everything in his former world had always been dependable and sufficient. Until now that is. Until the *event* had started, and one after another, unusual things began happening faster and faster, replacing contentment with anxiety. What had always happened in a predictable order and relationship changed. *Everything* changed, and he was baffled, bewildered, frightened and angry. Yes, he was angry. *Very* angry. He screamed and sound issued from him, something as alien to him as his new universe in frustration and anger, and, in the end, it didn't help.

Yet, after what had been no less than an eternity of unfaltering support and sustenance, he had, as his various senses gradually appeared and he began to use them to explore his collectively supportive world, been forced to notice that that both he and his world had, in fact, *always* been changing. Subtly. Over time. Well before the *event*: a little less room here, a tingling or pressure there, the pink aura surrounding him growing slowly brighter, a growing sense of concern he couldn't quite place. Of these feelings and sensations, however, it was his gradually growing awareness of smell that intrigued him most.

Earlier, taste had revealed that the liquid world all about him was uniformly salty, with a slowly increasing sourness. Though his lungs, mouth and nostrils remained comfortably filled with this liquid, when smell appeared, he became aware of a sweet-sharp smell, which he decided must be himself. More recently, however, even that smell had begun changing.

At first, for brief periods of times, the smells about him became particularly intense and infinitely varied. This sudden, piquant kaleidoscope of smells was always presaged by loud rumbles and gurgles just outside his world that, after a while, would be followed by a sudden feeling of energetic well-being within, eventually mollifying him into a somniferous state of bliss. Although he could never determine what these periodic smell-rushes were—perhaps yet another gift from whence he had inexplicably come?—this newly discovered change in his otherwise regular and heretofore highly predicable life suggested to him even back then a particularly disquieting feeling: that he was not alone. The sudden smells were clearly not him. They came from something outside not only of him, but also of the protective cocoon about him that was growing ever thinner, tougher and more resilient.

He also noticed another distinctive pattern. It usually occurred after the ruddy glow that encased him dimmed to quiet darkness. It was inevitably followed by a feeling of internal pressure, changing his perceived orientation from normal feet-up-head down to a less comfortable sideways position. When it happened, it occasionally presaged a change from the way things were, in his opinion supposed to be, to what he had taken to calling "Special Sideways Time."

Special Sideways Time typically began with soft "outside" rustlings, and then an inexplicable suffusion of deeper, more sonorous sounds interleaving with the more familiar, regular, higher-pitched melodious one to which he had become accustomed since, well, since as far back as he could recall. The two sounds often traded back and forth, sometimes harmoniously, other times dysharmoniously. The ever-present thump-hiss, thump-hiss, thump-hiss in the background would then increase in speed and intensity. On some occasions, the sounds would be accompanied by a feeling of firm rhythmic pressure. The infrequent though repetitious pressure, barely perceptible at first, would typically increase in intensity and speed then abruptly stop, exciting him to the point of kicking, butting or thrusting his body in synchrony. He loved the rocking and the building anticipation of the feeling of warmth and succor that inevitably followed. It was a giddy, whole-body feeling that made him curl his fingers and toes, the dreamy kind of feeling that instructed him to mirror the subsequent stillness and quiet and remain absolutely still. Special Sideways Time always left him feeling whole, complete, safe and at peace. But what he liked most about these times were the new smells.

They began with a rich, rank, spicy odor that permeated the liquid medium surrounding him, as if a third something—something pungent and urgent that was not of himself or the divine one he sensed was always watching over him—had suddenly dived uninvited into his private ocean. The smell rapidly intensified until it became bitingly sharp, almost acrid. By the time the rocking began, the smell would tingle his nose, peaking when the rocking stopped, to be inevitably followed by a rush of sharper, stronger, zestier and infinitely more provocative smells, just before the euphoria set in. Often he would just lay still, suspended in time and space, wallowing in wave after wave of pleasurable sensations and smells coursing through and suffusing him.

Chapter 2

Without reason, the cocoon that had always surrounded him, cuddling and protecting him in its forever nestling embrace, shuddered and began gripping him, ultimately forcing his body into a fixed alignment with the top of his head mashed against a hard, unremitting resistant wall. He remained that way for an interminable time, until a sudden loud pop sounded. That was, by his reckoning, when the singular *event* officially began. He could still recall with a shudder the painful flexing of his neck, forcing the top of his head forward and to the right as the protective cocoon grasped his body and changed to a deathly grip, jamming his head solidly into what turned out to be a far too narrow space that, until this moment, he hadn't even known existed. He gulped in surprise, opening his eyes for the first time in terror. He was trapped. He couldn't move, and he panicked.

After what seemed an eternity, the intense grip relaxed, apparently on its own, providing a brief respite. Exhausted and bewildered, he noticed to his horror that the firm walls about him were now closer and harder than before. While he tried desperately to adjust to his new, more compact world, the same walls began once again to grip him, vice-like and unyielding. This time, he was forced to fold his arms and legs tight against his chest. As the pressure began squeezing his temples, ramming the back of his head further into the narrow passageway, he could smell fear all about him, and it was erasing every other thought. While clearly *his* fear, it was somehow now mixed with that of another, and while the second smell inexplicably comforted him, it left him feeling frightened, abandoned and alone. Adding to his sense of nascent fear, the familiar thump-hiss-thump-hiss thump-hiss background sounds had become louder, faster, and inexplicably more distant. From far outside his imploding world he heard a wail like he had never heard before—it must be, he surmised, the wail of his omnipotent protector—accompanied by a growing cacophony of new sounds.

Abandoned by his protector, he knew for the first time the unbounded dread of loosing everything he had known including himself.

The world about him convulsed again, this time, smashing his face and nose against the slowly remitting tunnel while the cocoon surrounding the rest of his body closed relentlessly in. It was a defining moment that he would never forget. But the worst was the long, haunting wail that was slowly turning his fear into blind terror.

Chapter 3

Draff Rob Brie [Septican-Smite] was indignantly thrust out of the kind protective world of his mother's womb into an inexplicable world that literally reeked of new and terrifying smells. It all made no sense. It was a new world entirely out-of-control—an assault of riotous sensations: obnoxious smells, blaring sounds, and an explosion of perplexing lights.

Exhausted, suffocated, famished, he added his own wail to the tumultuous racket about him, grabbing for something—anything warm, protective, confining—but there was nothing. With growing foreboding, he pulled in his arms and legs, while at the same moment a sharp, stabbing pain ripped through his belly. This new world, for that's what it had to be, seemed like a malignantly discordant abyss inhabited by a constantly moving swirl of hazy, meaningless, painfully intense colors, a cacophony of noises and an unending procession of discordant smells. In short, it was a cold heartless world without succor. The rhythmic thump-hiss was no more. Torn forever from all that had protected and nurtured him, he felt only aloneness—true, utter aloneness—while every sense continued to wildly explode.

Yet even as the whirlwind of overwhelmining sensations continued its relentless attack, a singular, exotic smell caught his attention and, intriguing him, helped him regain a feeling of control. It was the familiar but stronger and more refined smell of his former world, his god, his protector, his mother, definite though diluted by competing sensations. It was, however, recognizable enough to make him turn his head, and in doing so, receive a comforting reward: a soft, warm, graspable mound offering nourishment, and with it, a regained sense of contentment. If this were to be his only succor, he would seize it and suckle for his very life.

Chapter 4

It was about this time that the newborn Draff Rob Brie [Septican-Smite], swaddled in a coarse dry blanket rather than the familiar but bygone ocean of warmth, realized that any hope of return to his former, decidedly more contemplative life was never to be. Nourished, surrounded by the safe smell of his mother, he fell into a deep sleep, to be interrupted a short time later—how long, who knew?—to awaken on a cold surface under a blinding white light, strapped spread-eagled on his back, frightened and wailing, while vague unfamiliar deep-voiced beings enshrouded in white and emitting frighteningly different smells, poked and prodded at a part of him located somewhere between his recently cut and still aching bellybutton and his legs struggling against bindings. He tried to squirm when a sharp, evil-smelling, cold, wet liquid was brushed all around this newly discovered, singular part. Struggle being futile, he tried without success to focus his eyes on the huge monstrosity commanding his entire visual field, sniffing in vain for the protective smell of his mother.

Suddenly, a searing bolt of pain, beginning at the tip of his singular part ripped though his body, making him reflexively strain at his bonds and scream as never before. The pain was not unlike what he'd felt in the center of his belly not long after being forced from his mother's womb but exponentially more intense. *How long ago had that been?* he wondered, as the pain slowly receded to an intense throbbing. In this new and malevolent universe, it was impossible to know.

He screamed and screamed in helpless agony, the loud and familiar thump-hiss, thump-hiss, thump-hiss of his beneficent former life replaced by a palpable and at the moment infinitely faster thut-thut-thut-thut-thut-thut-thut-thut emanating from his very center.

It would be some time before he could make any sense of what had and was continuing to happen to him in this new world. For the moment, he assumed that during the *event*, for having attempted desperately to hold onto some portion of his former universe's life-force, he had been cast from paradise, slapped roundly on his backside for his hubris, had his mouth and nose forcibly sucked out for his screaming, his body *twice* cut to make a point of his ill behavior, and was then thrown into a singularly hellacious place mitigated only by the intermittent provision of liquid nurture. In a moment's time, he had become a shadow of his former and now highly missed and increasingly appreciated self. It was as if this new place were bent on torturing him. And for what? For trying to hold onto even the smallest reminder of his former self and world?

It slowly occurred to him that the beating sound he was feeling within must be a vestige of the all-encompassing central life force upon which his current existence now wholly depended. That much, at least, he knew for certain. So, if the life force had changed, it had to be his perception of...time...yes, that was it...time had somehow become confused during the event. Whatever the cause, the result was devastating.

The intense, dull throbbing pain in his twice-cut outside central area continued, refusing to lessen. *What insanity* Brie thought, screaming again loudly, demanding in the most authoritative manner he knew. *Why won't all these horrible outside things just stop, disappear, leave?* Even as the as yet impossible to fully verbalize question coalesced within his agonized mind, he knew the answer: Succor didn't matter in this new world. Unlike his old world, this new one was not his, and despite, or perhaps because of all the agony and pain that existed about him, he needed to learn as quickly as possible how to navigate and survive in this new reality where *his* existence seemed of little import. Why did everything have to become so unpredictable, and, more so, unpredictably painful? *Why? Why? Why?*

His mental agonizing reawakened memories of the episode of overwhelming terror he'd experienced earlier. Was what he had just experienced a prelude to yet another impending transition, for transition it was, from one world to another completely different one? Could he *survive* another transition? Without being aware of it, Brie's mind slipped from troubled consciousness into blissful sleep, only to be re-thrust yet again into the crazy, alternately painful and yet— he had to admit—incredibly intriguing world in which he was now a prisoner.

When Brie awoke, as he preferred, unclothed, in his mother's warm, all encompassing embrace, to her familiar smell filling his nostrils, to her soft cooing calming his ragged nerves, a touch to his cheek was all that was needed to turn and reach out for the now familiar breast and began sucking intensely. Forcing from memory the nightmares that periodically interjected between his moments with his mother, the residual pain in his newly found and damaged but healing belly and pelvic appendage, the whole indignity of it all finally, gradually, diminished.

As he sucked, warm nutrient fill his belly, and his mind began drifting back, as it invariably did whenever he relaxed, to his life before the *event*. He'd been totally satisfied, when he was viciously attacked without reason. He hurt. Tears that couldn't yet be formed welled in the corners of his eyes, and he sucked harder trying to fight it all back, asking, praying to the huge embodiment of comfort cradling him for help. *Please help! PLEASE!*

Yet he had already come to realize that no one source in this new world, even the other apparently benevolent caretaker who occasionally stroked his brow while he was feeding and whose deeper voice sounded so familiar, could entirely comfort him. His sleepy mind recognized this second familiar voice as being from his increasingly distant past, before whatever it was he had done to be cast outside, helpless against the evil forces that inhabited and seemingly controlled this new world. Thoughts exploded in his head as he lay sucking ever stronger and more intently, absorbing every iota of nourishment, support and love he could in preparation for whatever challenges would invariably come next—and something unexpectedly painful *would* come, sooner or later, of that, he had no doubt. But he would never forget that monstrous white being floating over him with its deep, discordant voice and sharp astringent smell that had inflicted such pain with total indifference. He would never forget that smell just before he'd been twice cut. He'd never forget the rage he felt at being restrained. Or the mind-wrenching, sharp, searing pain in the tip of his appendage that seemed to last forever and, even now that the worst was over, refused to leave him entirely. Nor would he ever forget this place or the smell of fear, his own and his mother's, and that of the demonic beasts that inhabited this new world.

Sucking harder, he determined to hold tightly to the knowledge that he could trust only one thing in this crazy world: the smell of his mother; the only constant upon which he could depend. Well, not the only one: While eyes, ears, mouth and skin were constantly being deceived, "the nose always knows."

Given that, he had begun noticing his mother's smell subtly changing based on his actions and reactions, and, to his utter surprise, to their combined actions and reactions to the seemingly infinite number of demons constantly popping into and out of his limited visual field. In the end, Draff Rob Brie [Septican-Smite] learned there was only one sense he could always rely on, but he worried if, like his former world and now his mother's smell, it, too, would change and might eventually betray him.

Chapter 5

The cautious, gifted infant so impudently thrust into this new and highly perplexing world would eventually come to learn that his social family name, Septican-Smite, was not to be lightly shared. He would learn that people— and there were an increasing number appearing daily in his new world whom he could identify by smell—no longer maintained biological family names or, for that matter, biological family ties. Using a biological rather than social family name like Septican-Smite was, in fact, widely considered an assaultive act meant to foster discriminatory dependency. It was not just discouraged, it was, he would even later discover, *unconstitutional* to reveal, if it hadn't already been wiped entirely from memory. This was taken deadly seriously by *special* individuals for whom he, too, would quickly develop an innate fear: Enforcers. People these days had four names, but instead of using, revealing or even knowing their biological father or mother's names, the inhabitants of this new world all had a formal social family name (typically, one based on the names of one's first custodians) for use by strangers and new acquaintances; then a "common" tag for use in social situations or when being reprimanded; then a "normative" handle strictly for use by friends; and finally a first or "intimate" name for use by those with whom he would likely someday mate. He was, therefore, "Septican-Smite" when first introduced to someone new, and "Brie" whenever he did something wrong. He was "Rob" to his friends and custodians when good, and he was "Draff" to those with whom he was or hoped to someday be physically intimate: Draff Rob Brie [Septican-Smite].

Second in importance to smell, he valued his ability to speak. Smell told him almost everything he needed to know, but speaking gave him control over what ever it was he smelled. He'd been in the new world almost one-and-a-half years before the ability to speak words finally came to him, which by every reckoning, was unusually early.

Having just been corrected for fidgeting by one of his pair of custodians, he ventured, "I Brie. Live..."—the "in" part always gave him trouble—"...Emory-Shi," he recounted shakily as he'd had been taught to say at two years of age whenever asked by a stranger or an Enforcer...*in Shica Centro, Illi Prefecture, NewAmerica,* he wished he could add, but at two-and-a-half, the six additional words would have hopelessly entangled him and, if it was an Enforcer, likely piqued unwanted further attention. As it was, it would have been far too bold a statement had he uttered all he was thinking, anyway. Brie was surprised when his and the other boy's custodians, upon hearing Brie's attempted introduction, smiled and moved several feet away, leaving the two boys alone with each other.

Though unable to do so, Brie felt compelled to further explain who he was to the boy standing in front of him with his arms crossed, his eyebrows fixed in a threatening V-shape and his eyes locked on Brie. The boy waited, his putative name, Frunk, having been shouted out loudly a moment before by a frowning custodian for the same crime of brevity as Brie. Technically, both boys lived in Emory-Shi, "Shi" meaning "new" (a designation as commonly in use these days as dropping articles like "the" when speaking) given that so much of NewAmerica was, in fact, new. Emory was an officially recognized community of the new government capital, Chicago, concatenated in NewSpeak to "Chica." While there were, at first, significantly fewer states after the reorganization, now there were none. Neither boy therefore felt the need to concern himself with the former name of the former state in which he now lived, the states having been cleverly replaced by the government with less powerful, more easily controlled and not uncommonly unspoken "communities."

Frunk, previously unknown to Brie, appeared similar

in height, weight and demeanor, each being particularly bright and curious. Given their similarities and the way their custodians had moved away from them, it seemed, even to toddler Brie, unlikely this first meeting was serendipitous.

Brie, to be more precise, was not just bright, he was uniquely aware—fully so—from his time in the womb to present. He was also aware that because of this and his heightened sense of smell, he was different from most other children. Everyone, including his custodians, agreed early on that he was well above being simply exceptionally bright, as there was, in addition, his gift of being able to remember things particularly well (though, in fact, his near eidetic memories were all associated with a smell—he *never* forgot a smell or any event associated with it).

His awareness, intelligence, memory and gift of smell made him exceptionally curious, which made him stand blatantly out even from other unusually gifted children, and this heightened curiosity was constantly getting him in trouble. From his perspective, it wasn't curiosity at all. What he really sought was to simply know how things that had a scent in this new world did what they did, where they came from, and what, in essence, it and everything "meant."

His biggest curiosity at this moment was Frunk and another child standing beside and slightly behind Frunk— more specifically why the two happened to be there at all. The second child, of similar exceptional presence, introduced herself after Frunk to Brie as Jan. Awkward introductions finally aside, without further discussion (following a brief sniff of the Frunk and Jan by Brie) the three became playmates.

Frunk, it soon became apparent, was the loudest and boldest. His dark-skinned, finely featured face was haloed by a tousle of tight black curls. He was curious like Brie, but unlike Brie, never hesitated before announcing a new discovery. To Brie, he smelled of warm, robust forest. Playing next to each other, mutually sharing anything and everything that happened to catch their interests, they would have been, in others' eyes, destined to become the closest of friends, which was exactly what their respective custodians planned.

Jan sat quietly beside Frunk copying his every move like a small clone, until, clearly bored, she stood, walked towards Brie and plopped down between the two boys. Jan was not only the smallest of the three, she was thinner and quieter. Her long, silky-brown hair and huge, liquid-brown eyes made her look like an evanescent doe. Her bare, lightly-colored limbs and legs contrasted like vanilla against Frunk's swarthy, milk chocolate and Brie's olive-colored skin. If Frunk smelled of spicy forest, Jan smelled of fresh spring rain, and, sitting between Frunk and

Brie, the two smelled to Brie of a freshly wetted forest of exceptional fullness and character. Positioned between the boys, Jan watched Brie intensely while deferring to Frunk. Brie *should* have felt…what? Affronted? Confused? Angry? But there was something about the way haughty Jan stared, invitingly, almost alluringly askance, at Brie that told him, along with her smell, that she, too, would prove a lifelong friend, different from, but equally important to him as Frunk.

When Jan inserted herself between them, she immediately became engrossed in Frunk and Brie's attempts to establish a name for an object that Frunk produced. It was a friendly contest between the two boys, in part to share in the discovery and in part to establish social dominance, Frunk unknowingly, and Brie with full awareness of what he was doing, but with little understanding of why. Jan, watching, listening, observing each, abruptly reached out a delicate arm, grabbed the object from the two, and, tossing her hair at Brie, presented it to him, firmly repeating Frunk's name for it. For some inexplicable reason, this singular action settled the contest, leaving Brie the unacknowledged leader and Frunk, his decisive second-in-command, with Jan asserting herself within the newly formed threesome as arbiter. From that moment forward and without any further discussion, Brie became the decision-maker whenever a novel rational solution was required, Frunk when a practical, physical or mechanical solution was needed, and Jan whenever the situation was unclear. It was at this moment they became a mob.

It should be noted that their first meeting was quite unusual for the times; which was exactly what the three's custodians who'd removed themselves a short distance away, were, at that very moment, avidly discussing. That is, the threesome's meeting had occurred "in the flesh," when, by all conventions and for innumerable health and safety reasons, it should have been holographic. From each's perspective, the other two should have appeared as holographic projections so vivid that the two projections would have had partial though highly convincing physical substance.

It should also be noted that, generally speaking, only Enforcers these days wore clothes. This particular situation, and the fact that their custodians were not immediately there to intervene, inevitably led them, *sans* clothes, to explore each other, the gist of their adventure being that Brie discovered with surprise that Jan had no extra crotch finger; Frunk discovered he and Brie had more in common than they'd first thought, and Jan discovered that she was proudly different from the two boys. Jan also discovered that to make the block of wood she was holding stack on top of several others would require a larger block at the bottom of the stack to keep them all from falling over. This latter discovery quickly captured their combined interest.

Chapter 6

Brie, now eight years old, had completed three years of directed home study largely by holographic classes, and had heard countless times from one after another naked holographic interactive instructor that he and his nest mates, Frunk, now called by Brie by his more familiar name, Frann, and Jan, similarly now called by Brie and Frann, Andry, together constituting their mob, along with several less central new additions, had been selected to become an "educational group." Exactly who or what had made this determination was a mystery even to their custodians, but it was a significant act, as was the fact that their new set of holographic instructors suddenly became world class, something reserved for only a select few.

Unknown to them, in the early twenty-first century, the former United States of America had been forced into dissolution by its then President, Alexander Mathias Jackson, who had immediately resurrected it into the smaller, leaner, more robust NewAmerica which, in the end, was about half the size of its former self. The "old" USA with its odd social quirks resulting largely from its increasingly strongly anti-humanistic emphasis on "making money" (as if one could physically "make money," it being, at that same time, quixotically illegal to literally do so) was now largely regarded by NewAmericans as an historical oddity relegated little student study-time, and then mostly in passing. It was upon NewAmerica that their lessons were focused, a topic equally dry to the educational group of twelve whose real interest was more in getting through the lesson so they could return to individually playing.

NewAmerica was founded on a revisioning of the phrase, "Yankee trade with a twist," as government Advertisers, what "G-men" and the populace called "Gadvertisers." What restarted small, ended up quickly surpassing all the former nation's glories: NewAmerica with its primary focus on global trade had proven, after a difficult start, so economically successful that most of the planet was now contractually owned or at least obligated to NewAmerica.

In response, former nations of any consequence had had to flee to, colonize, claim or control a planet or at least an orbiting space community of their own in order to preserve what they could of their culture and survive economically. Still, ever since the Great Diaspora, most if not all off-worlders retained a soft spot in their heart for

Mother Earth. This, in spite of the fact that due to gradual space adaptation, many of the billions upon billions of emigrants now living on the myriad non-Earth gravity planets like Rus', NewMoo and Chin' would never be able to physically return to Mother Earth. For the lucky few who could, NewAmerica's Gadvertisers were constantly touting Earth as the mythical Origin and principal Gathering Place of Humanity, enticing them to pilgrimage at least once in a lifetime back to their "common roots." In the process, NewAmerica would carefully relieve the pilgrims of the burden of their lifesavings. In this manner, visitors religiously and practically contributed to the maintenance of the Cradle of Humankind. In return, Mother Earth (more correctly NewTerra though essentially a globalized NewAmerica), acknowledged and constantly promoted this special kind of what it called "core" tourism. Profits from this venture—and they were astronomical—made NewTerra an ever more attractive destination to off-worlders who typically lived under the worst conditions imaginable. As such, NewAmerica and its public face, NewTerra, continued to set the desired standard of living for humans everywhere.

As their new instructor-hologram droned on, Brie, now Rob to Frann and Andry, mocked the image, silently mouthing its words to hide his own thoughts, uncertain whether the huge, God-like, frighteningly palpable image hovering in the air before him could, as custodians everywhere constantly reminded their wards, read his every thought. In Brie's opinion, NewAmerica/NewTerra/Mother Earth had done pretty well given the total meltdown from which it had emerged.

As a consequence of their current instructor's repetitious presentation of one after another NewAmerican historical events, Brie—still Brie to his instructors—came slowly to understand that most democracies, pure, or mixed like the former USA, couldn't and didn't last long. Even the former USA, with its clever built-in checks and balances and all its initial accumulated wealth ultimately fell, depending as all nations did on the honesty, empathy and resolution of its leaders and, ultimately, its people. From what he had heard so far, Americans, especially their elected leaders, had failed democracy and their nation in all three aspects.

Whether from laziness, ignorance, greed, or fad, like a mortal human, the death of the USA and its form of democracy had always been lurking impatiently just below the surface—waiting for its people to make one, final, outrageous blunder. Life, the projected hologram before him reminded, was different now.

At his tender age, Brie alone of his educational group was aware that life as he knew it was being subtly but persistently programmed in his mind by the underlying government through their instructors. What the rest of his group were principally aware of was that the process, whatever its goal, seemed unchangingly boring. Yet at the same time, from what Brie could ascertain, he, his nest mates or mob, his new educational group and, through them, NewAmerica's residents had been granted a reprieve, a moment in the sun, an opportunity for a fresh start, inviting them individually and collectively to redeem themselves by constantly redefining, implementing and re-sculpting a new future for NewAmerica, NewTerra and the human-colonized universe.

Mother Earth, like him, was actually thriving after barely surviving the total meltdown. In his mind, this was not so much a conclusion extracted from the holographic history instructor's defense of NewAmerica and NewDemocracy, but the heroic results of three historical flesh-and-blood saints (or revolutionaries depending on one's personal point-of-view): Adelphous Tripler, Shawn Clarke and Amelie Stewart, who, from Brie, Frunk and Jan's perspectives, represented the collective future.

Brie yawned and looked lazily at the far wall whose perceptibly changing color reflected the time of day, hoping the mere act of looking and yawning would somehow make time and the color change go faster. In truth, he was also interested in catching the attention of his mob. While each individual in the educational group was listening more or less attentively in his or her own home to the same hypnotic lecture, each's presence was also being projected holographically and interactively around his or her instructor so that, from each educatee's perspective, they were actually all together, sitting at their instructor's feet, enraptured by his enlightening utterances. Brie desperately wanted to find out what was up with Frann and Andry. Technically, the central hologram couldn't *do* anything outright to stop him from asking (at least that's what he wanted to believe), but, he cautiously reminded himself, it was unwise to trust holograms that *might* be able to read minds that had no smell, and if there was one thing he'd learned during his short life in this world, it was that he couldn't trust anything or anyone that had no smell.

Chapter 7

My mob, Brie was dreamily thinking when he abruptly realized that all eyes, including the holographic instructor's, were fixed on him. Brie looked at the seemingly solid images of the members of his educational group spread about him, and blushed at the sudden rush of laughs, finger-pointings and catcalls directed at him. A feeling of anxiety seized and swept through him, making him suddenly, crave their actual, individual, physical presence, particularly that of Frunk, who, unlike the others, was fidgeting awkwardly with some new pan-digital device that had momentarily captured his attention, and Jan, who was staring wide-eyed at Brie while watching Frunk's holographic image silently out of the corner of her eyes. What was it Brie saw flicker in her gaze before she returned her attention to Frunk? This had become one of Brie's newest and most intriguing curiosities. Physically separated from his inner circle since the threesome's first meeting, this particular curiosity was gradually becoming an obsession. He *needed* to be physically beside Frann and Andry. He needed not just to *see* their presences, but to *smell* them. Though he couldn't put his mental finger on it, there was also something more he needed—craved—to know…

"After Total Meltdown, Mother Earth's denizens…" the distant, yet surprisingly realistic, unclothed projection of their teacher began as if oblivious to the educatees' pointings, snickers and fidgeting's, "…quickly began identifying as NewAmericans and in gradually increasing numbers as NewTerrans. These days, NewAmerica and NewTerra, while already anachronisms—illusory, brackish, literary by-waters of our past—remain rooted in NewSpeak. Everything today is valued primarily for its novelty, and whatever epicurean or hedonistic pleasures that accompany it. Only that which can be brought into being, evolved, trademarked, packaged, distributed and sold in interplanetary marketplaces retains any semblance of actual newness."

Their instructor continued to drone on, adroitly dropping articles as customary in NewSpeak. "Nowadays, whenever sellable ideas, products, gadgets or commodities are identified on NewTerra, Gadvertisers quickly make certain that every emigrant takes with him or her embedded desires to possess it (and, of course, every other NewTerran idea, product, gadget or commodity so carefully associated in their minds with 'home' or, more specifically, 'Mother

Earth'). This approach created an epidemic-scale galactic 'dis-ease'—deep, unconscious longings to possess tokens of Mother Earth. This construct centerpieced NewTimes global entrepreneurship, protecting and at same time enriching Mother Earth/NewTerra/NewAmerica with fruits of desires of her billions of spawn scattering throughout the universe."

Bries' mob would later learn that the desire to return 'home' and spend most of a colonist's wealth on NewTerra was physically embedded into each colonist's DNA through individual epigenetic manipulation, resulting in an overwhelming urge similar to that which caused salmon to return to the stream where they had been hatched. This change was introduced during the "training program" which all future colonists were required to attend before being allowed to travel off world.

It's always about contro, contro, contro, thought Brie with irritation. *Thanks to this one simple advance, NewTerra has become flush with contro—the modern name for interplanetary mammon—what in the old days used to be called 'money'.*

"So why, if Terra is so prosperous," Brie asked aloud, "is everyone always leaving?"

The instructor's monologue abruptly stopped as if considering Brie's question, then continued its lecture in a typically obtuse answer: "NewAmerica today, through its monopolistic government control of Chica-to-Orbital-Space Tether, Nev Orbital Space Plane and both Hawai and P-Rican Interplanetary Heavy Launch facilities, quite effectively controls humanity and its future. One must remember that immediately after Total Meltdown, nothing at local, state, national or international level worked. To make things worse, the next generation, stripped of everything familiar, was unable to manage and maintain what people and resources remained. Everyone looked to United Nations—now the United People's Ancestors, what we today colloquially call 'UPA' or simply 'Up' for short—to re-establish some semblance of governance, economy and social order. Everything 'Up', however, was kept functionally impotent through clever machinations by then President Jackson. In end, as if in reward for its impotence, Up was awarded control of a portion of land on NewTerra independent of NewAmerican control."

Was that the source of the ubiquitous greeting, 'Up yours'?" Brie wondered, chuckling to himself. Apparently not all holographic instructors can read minds, Brie concluded, as this one totally ignored his impertinent thought-aphorism and simply droned on.

"Up was ceded entire former Eastern Seaboard including former Washington D.C.—now Wash-shi—where Up's hundred-square-mile headquarters complex is currently located. Ceded lands also included former New York—now York-shi—where most Up bureaucrats now live, and former Cape Bold, known back then as Cape Canaveral, NewTerra's only Public Interplanetary Travel site or 'PIT Stop' as people now call it."

Brie forced a smile at what he assumed was an attempt at artificial intelligence humor. It was impossible to tell with instructional holographs. A real human would have emitted a smell that would have confirmed it instantly. What he did know from previous instruction was that everyone who could afford it traveled NewAmerican, and only those who couldn't took their chances at PIT-stop facilities. If, that is, they could secure Up travel clearance; wade through the legions of callous bureaucrats reluctant to add his or her required signature-stamp (unless, of course, sufficient contro were unobtrusively placed in an open palm); and a reasonable chance existed that the person would still be alive by the time of the next available public launch. Back then, and even today, waiting times at PIT-stops were typically ten to fifteen years, and, despite Gadvertiser's claims to the opposite, the wait times never decreased.

Why would anyone ensconce him or herself to Up for the opportunity of dying in a rusting, public rocket-coffin? Brie turned the image of a rusting coffin over in his mind, after a while adding aloud with an audible laugh, "It's the

Pits!"

Those who, like Brie, continued living on Mother Earth by choice and were willing to accept the system for what it was, were inclined to praise, revere, even worship Jackson, Tripler, Clarke and Stewart, the four almost mythical political icons who, together, had fearlessly recreated NewAmerica/NewTerra into what it was today.

Their instructor's history of the ever-increasing legendary foursome—former United States of America President Jackson, and Tripler, Clarke and Stewart—was a bedtime story told and retold to every child on every colonized planet. Brie, once again bored, reached lazily up and pretended to tousle the instructor holograph's flaming orange hair. His mob and the entire educational group suddenly came alive when he then provocatively caressed the instructor's green-rouged cheeks and naughtily licked the image's long, ochre-tinted fingertips before kneeling back down and bowing at the naked image's feet. Brie hoped everyone saw and enjoyed his visual statement, but, in truth, what he really wanted to do was dash out of the projected classroom, right now, with his mob alongside him, leaving behind the rest of the educational group.

How many times do I have to be reminded that it was humankind's 'manifest destiny' to fully exploit not just Mother Earth, but the entire solar system and surrounding universe as well? It was what he, his mob and countless other mobs and educational groups on NewTerra were being inculcated to believe, and he assumed it was his gift of unusually strong conscious presence that gave him the insight to question it, which few if any of his fellow educatees seemed to do. Still, this spectacularly *largesse* concept was, sadly, not of his origin and thereby not of over-riding interest.

Too bad, Brie thought dreamily to himself. *If I'd have thought of it earlier and had foresight enough to register my idea with the government, I would be fabulously rich.* The idea of humankind having a singular purpose—that purpose being *to be exploited for a minority of humanity's profit and indulgent enjoyment*—was fervently and unconsciously believed by most young, get-rich-quick, NewTime entrepreneurs—Fast Eddies as they were infamously called these days—and almost everyone these days, including Brie, was a Fast Eddie if for no other reason simply by virtue of being alive. In fact, everyone these days *had* to be a Fast Eddie. Cleverness had become the most highly prized, eagerly sought and bounteously rewarded human attribute, and Brie, at the least, could easily imagine himself as others constantly reminded him, a very clever and ultimately very, very rich young man.

A sudden loud yell broke his reverie. "Brie!" the

holographic instructor yelled, placing a ruddy hand on its hip, the other hand pointing a brick red, long-nailed, index finger accusingly at him. Everyone in the educational group about him quieted anxiously; then, after a short but respectful silence, resumed their former giggles, laughs, pointings and catcalls, Frann-Frunk leading the melee while Andry-Jan looked on fretfully.

For his part, Brie, scowling, stood, folded his arms on his chest and leaned his back unrepentantly against a wall, shifting his weight nonchalantly onto one leg to emphasize his disdain and being above it all, while at the same time, through the gesture, attempting to reassert his leadership of both his mob and the educational group. Aware of Brie's act of defiance, Andry shifted her gaze from Frann to Rob/Brie, slid back into the far fringes of the holographic group, and, wide-eyed, licked her lips wetly then stuck out her tongue while sliding her hands slowly down her naked sides.

Other than Brie, no one noticed her action, the group's attention being fixed at that moment solidly on Brie. As soon as the raucous laughter died, the instructor, unruffled, resumed his monologue. Nevertheless, everyone's eyes remained on Brie, while his were locked on Andry and the holographic image of her slender, naked, stunningly inviting female body barely discernible in the unfocused distance.

Chapter 8

That day, something changed between the three. Andry continued watching the two boys, always placing herself nearer Frann and siding with him in most issues, but her glances at Rob/Brie seemed to Brie to have become more prolonged, as if in that moment she were trying to find something in him that she had long ago discovered in Frann. Rob shook his head to clear the swirl of charged but disconnected thoughts exploding in his head. What did he really care what Andry did or thought of him? Nothing had *physically* changed. They were still nest mates and still members of the same mob, of which he was still the tacit leader. They were as close to being brothers or sisters as was possible in these NewTimes, where the very concept of *familia* and all the discriminatory control and discretely hidden violence that historically accompanied it were openly being replaced by the existence of NewTimes nests.

It wasn't until later, when at twelve years, Rob formally started preparing for his liberation from that nest that he finally put together what was being fed to his and all the other mobs by the different holo-instructors and was, as a result, changing them. Honing, pruning, re-integrating, seizing possession of everything he'd learned, he piece-by-piece reconstructed all he'd been taught within his mind into a single cohesive narrative.

It was then he became aware of how far NewAmerica had come from the Malthusian nightmare of the pre-Meltdown decade when, as predicted, people's survival needs had, quite simply, outstripped planetary resources, and people began dying prematurely beneath the hooves of the Biblical Four Horsemen of the Apocalypse: War, Famine, Pestilence and Revenge of the Wild Beasts (or, as a recent instructor recontextualized using the pre-Meltdown philosopher-prophet Gottman's reversion: Criticism, Contempt, Defensiveness and Stonewalling). In their desperation, people were only too glad to give up personal freedoms for work. Anything for work and the perception of safety. Any work that would secure enough contro for them to stay alive for another day, or in NewAmerica and Rob and his mob's special case, continue to enjoy their carefree, hedonistic, adolescent lifestyle for yet awhile longer.

Rob recalled one of his later custodians—he'd had many, though most youth his age only had the initial pair or at most one more—say that trading individual freedoms for contro was a necessary segue into the world of the multi-corporate government aristocracy that had been carefully nurtured and led from behind-the-scenes by former President-idol Jackson's arch nemesis, prior USA President Brown. Rob remembered the story well: The custodian had purportedly been one of Brown's aides (substitute the archaic word "henchmen") until Brown and his minions were isolated, arrested, rehabilitated and eventually repatriated. The current government, remaining wary of all such previous "brown-shirts," repatriated or not, still looked in periodically to make certain that Brie's albeit brief association with that particular personal custodian hadn't negatively affected his overall education.

The thought caused Rob to recall the words of their current history lecturer: "Brown created labyrinthine, petroleum-based, global corporate conglomerates to try to command what, from his perspective, was an increasingly crazed voting rabble. Slowly and insidiously, Brown recruited cadres of like-minded executives and managers willing to work tirelessly under his direction for absolute control, and that eventually bankrupted what was left of USA and brought about its implosion. Brown's misjudgment ushered in the nightmarish Total Meltdown, the full likes of which worlds will hopefully never experience again."

"Everyone," the instructor's voice continued in Rob/Brie's ears, "immediately prior to those somber times unconsciously knew USA was doomed. It was just that, like with former USSR, no one had courage to say it aloud."

I would have said it aloud, Rob thought, imagining himself Adelpheus Tripler, guns in both hands blazing, fighting legions of brown-shirt corporate executives lurking zombie-like about him.

The problem, Rob had slowly come to understand, was that any hope of avoiding the economic disaster disappeared on election eve when the defeated incumbent, President Brown, had called President-elect Jackson with his now infamous announcement that instead of acknowledging defeat, he was "abdicating." Brown knew if he stayed in office even a day longer, he would be arrested for what he'd done to the nation, and likely hauled out and executed by legions of disgruntled followers. Americans had found the hellish, though thankfully short, Total Meltdown that followed Brown's abdication with its weeks of foreign invasions and outbreak of civil war almost unbearable. Almost, because President-elect Jackson at last minute pulled off his Gorbachev-like emergency reorganization of the USA during the remaining seconds of the eleventh hour.

Despite Rob's outward cheekiness—his trademark "attitude" which he largely maintained for the mob though more recently he suspected equally for Andry—provided him just enough distance from the mass of information the eduatees in his educational group were being subjected to, to completely absorb, re-order and re-interpret his lessons. He understood, for example, that what had brought a quick end to the total meltdown had actually been an odd, seemingly serendipitous combination of events, not the least of which had been the sudden worldwide realization that while money had pushed the USA to the brink of crisis, no amount of it could save it from the looming meltdown. And melt down it did. Or so his educators held.

Knowing the government was bankrupt; money would no longer buy anything. This is what actually shook Americans to the point of armed rebellion and eventual civil war. Months after Jackson halted the attempted foreign invasions of the former states of Hawaii, Alaska, California and Texas, nipped the civil war in the bud and reorganized the faltering nation into the leaner, meaner, more robust NewAmerica sixty percent the size of the former USA, the cost of living still continued to escalate exponentially, while salaries, or "sally" as salaries were called now to distinguish them from contro which could be acquired unsystematically in a variety of ways—didn't. NewAmerica at that moment was eating itself alive while its inhabitants continued to starve.

Fixing the economy proved not just challenging, but literally impossible. Changing old America's perspective, in this case from an inward-looking, self-absorbed, self-satisfying, petroleum-and-automobile society to an outward-looking global participant with a cohesive, space-based vision had been President Jackson's most brilliant and most successful gambit. People today—even those who didn't eulogize Jackson—still revered him for it. Even so, everyone in these NewTimes was aware that it still might actually have been the sudden fortuitous appearance of several seemingly unrelated technologies that actually saved the fledgling NewAmerica and ultimately transformed it into the economic powerhouse it was today. Individually, these technologies would have never have likely come into existence or changed the nation, but with President Jackson leading the way, they catalyzed each other and NewAmerica emerged, ready to embrace an entirely new future.

Rob awoke from his mental recount of history as he envisioned it. Although he'd since heard the next part many times, it never ceased to amaze him in its retelling, and he, like everyone else, enjoyed a good story, true or not. Still, it was odd that the immense insights he felt he was suddenly gaining seemed to always point serendipitously back to that singular moment when, in the fringes of the hologram, Andry/Jan had licked her lips and stuck out her tongue at him, in his fertile mind for him and him alone.

Chapter 9

The first new technological event that yanked a commiserating very NewAmerica out of Total Meltdown was the invention of ContraSpray, a cheap and easily manufactured aerosol that temporarily inhibited ovulation and immunized users against sexually-transmitted diseases, while at the same time chemically encouraging sexual receptivity. Actually, it was simply an amazingly efficient combination of already known hormone-analogs, vaccines and pheromones instantly appreciated by an over-stressed populace and a government struggling to keep its citizenry mollified day-to-arduous-day while President Jackson's sweeping changes worked their slower magic. Although at first billed as a novelty, demand among youth, who saw little they could do to assist in the economic overhaul, was so high that it's manufacture, sale and use increased exponentially every subsequent month throughout the latter part of the meltdown. Of course, as people in increasing numbers fled Mother Earth, they carried their demand for the product with them. On NewTerra, its hefty price was gladly subsidized by NewAmerica, pleased to do anything that would decrease the birth rate (and thereby population), and move its residual citizenry away from reproducing or, in their economic misery, reverting back to conflict or civil war. Subsidized ContraSpray worked famously.

Because of ContraSpray, sex without the necessity of procreation or disease became an instant, universal rage. On NewTerra, it proved to be the true "opium of the masses" needed by the government to keep people working if only to obtain enough sally or contro to make their next ContraSpray purchase. It was a matter of temporarily replacing food with sex, fulfilling the desperate needs of the disenfranchised with fulfillment of their fantasies until the massive reorganization President Jackson was putting into place could solidify and take effect. What resulted was a harder-working yet surprisingly satisfied population. The immediately resulting negative population growth led to quick improvements in the quality of life. Fourteen-year-old Rob chortled under his breath as he always did when re-examining the descriptions by his instructors of the "early days" and the later, profound consequences of widespread ContraSpray use. *Why did it always take adults so long to see the obvious?*

The second technological innovation followed on the

heels of ContraSpray: Eugitors, invisible, molecular-thin second-skins that could project a luminous rainbow of hues unique to its inhabitant's immediate emotions. When slipped into, the Eugitor auto-located its built-in array of nanosensors into numerous key bodily areas, the wearers totally unaware of the unit constantly sampling their body chemistry. For enough contro, the nanosensors could be programmed to make and dispense small but surprisingly effective doses of hormone-inducers as well as a variety of other individualized proprietary drugs. With minimal (though decidedly very expensive) additional alteration, the units could also be made to respond to external stimuli. Wearers could, in essence, experience not only whatever part of their day-to-day lives they wished in a "heightened" and decidedly more pleasurable way, but also the sensations of any other person with whom the wearer came into contact in any way of the wearer's choosing, creating as friendly, romantic, erotic or off-putting an experience for both as desired. For example, a person wearing a "modified" Eugitor could choose to experience solitary or shared sex selectively in the prolonged pre-, mid- or post-state of orgasm. Wireless communication vendors immediately came up with options whereby one consenting wearer could not only experience, but also control another's experience from a distance. The majority of these body suits were made in one standard size and version, but rarer custom ones, like the one's Brie and many other privileged NewAmerican teens longed for, boasted additional amenities, like for instance, organic gill slits that allowed users to explore underwater environments while giving others sensory access to the wearer's water-environment-enhanced body sensations.

The third was CandyShades, a retail consumer device that looked for the most part like a pair of futuristic wrap-around designer sunglasses. The difference, however, was that CandyShades allowed one to visually enter a variety of virtual worlds of his or her choice, alone or with others. It was even possible to negotiate and program mutually agreed upon experiences. The NewAmerican government, riding the tsunami-wave of ContraSpray and Eugitor, immediately subsidized its own subscription version of CandyShades called CandyCable that could be wirelessly integrated into an employer's base unit system, subtly altering worker's perceptions, experiences and ultimately feelings and memories of their work even while working. CandyCable created an alternate reality that made work infinitely more palatable and satisfying. In response, the NewAmerican government *paid* citizens to subscribe, using the service to subtly, unconsciously "educate" wearers by virtual experience, for example, about various forms of labor consistent with the subscriber's particular abilities. It was touted by everyone as nothing less than a miracle, ultimately raising the formerly insipid work ethic to seraphic proportions.

"The rest, as they say, is history," Rob murmured under his breath, once again slipping back to the insistent vision of Andry/Jan in the misty distance, staring questioningly at him. Yet, to be completely honest, it wasn't really the vision of her that was haunting him. It was her unspoken question. It seemed inviting, stopping just short of an actual invitation. And despite all he had learned, all he knew, how quick he was at it and the unwavering loyalty given him by his mob, there was something *she* knew or had that he didn't. If only they had actually been in that room next to each other, he could have smelled and identified it. Instead the mystery remained, growing in his mind as if it had a life of its own, slowly consuming more of his day-to-day thoughts and attention.

Rob stared dejectedly down at his open palms, fingers interlaced, thumbs unconsciously but softly caressing each other in a circular dance. "That girl!" he said emphatically, dis-entwining his hands and shaking them roughly at his sides. As he did, hazy specters of more important matters that the vision of her had temporarily cast aside re-assembled on the fringes of his consciousness, vociferously demanding attention.

Where had he been moments ago in his recollection of the history of NewAmerica? Ah, the private sector. Not to be outdone by the government, private corporations entered into all-out competition offering shorter, more intense, more outrageous, more entertaining and ever more integrated combinations of ContraSpray, Eugitors, CandyShades and CandyCable—"T-rips" as they came to be called. The exact combination of technologies and their unique "mix" each private company employed in creating their signature T-rips quickly became the most valued trade secrets in the universe. In this era of Fast Eddies, many gambled, most lost and a few won at T-rip industrial espionage. Ungraciously called "double-oh-nothings," most of these wannabes, in the end, simply disappeared, leaving their nest mates to suffer the consequences of their short preoccupation in that outwardly admired, but socially despised and uniformly vilified occupation. "Today," in Rob/Brie's latest instructor's words, "hitherto forgotten human morality was slowly, albeit unconsciously reincarnating into a NewMorality based not solely on the contro or sally value of new products, but instead on effective *service* to other living creatures, including, in some outlier versions, to artificially intelligent—in NewSpeak, AI or "Eye"—pseudo-living machines.

As might be expected, these three key social

technologies (and others as well) sprang from a series of lesser-known scientific discoveries. One was the ability to chemically capture and later compose micro-fragments of human memories into new, fully fledged sensory experiences, whether the source was living or deceased, and whether human, animal, plant or more recently bacterial or "Eye" in origin. Such memories from anything but living-humans—surrogate or "Fake Memories" as they were street-called—could be cleverly constructed into natural- seeming memories, even of formerly-living-but-now-dead or even never-living things. The later spawned the creation of supposedly remembered eidetic-feelings by prior living and even non-living things of the past, present *and future*. A consumer of Fake Memories—FakeM's—exposed to just the right fragments in just the right sequence, when placed into a vivid actual or virtual situation—for example, *a la* Eugitor, CandyShades or Cable— would instantly recreate in the rememberer's minds a realistic-feeling memory that businesses could then package, market and resell to eager, ensconced consumers seeking the ultimate in passive entertainment. And make considerable contro for the corporation by doing so.

At first physically dangerous and of outrageous draw—the NewAmerican term for cost—simple hubris made these super-enhanced, memory-changing T-rips irresistible to bored youths biding their time in preparation for adulthood, citizenship and sallied work. These enhanced T-rips quickly replaced all other forms of desired adolescent entertainment.

Integrated into an enhanced, four-dimensional seven-sensory Eugitor—dubbed by the new generation a Forty-Seven Suit—one could, for example, remember or experience life as an ancient, now-extinct dinosaur, a two-thousand-year-old oak tree, a present day wolf, a future disease bacterium, even a timeless rock, this latter proving especially popular with the bolder elderly, especially when rapid social changes seemed overwhelming. Such a T-rip allowed them the sense of almost unlimited time to ponder what, if anything, might exist after death that was better than what there was now, and what, if anything, was inevitably awaiting them in the afterlife, if there was one.

Boring, Rob/Brie recalled mouthing simultaneously with the rest of the mob when the subject of dying came up, as it inevitably did with the older, less adaptable generation of holographic instructors.

Once, during a lesson when the subject of death was specifically addressed, Andry, who had become the subject of an increasing number of Rob's askance glances, boldly crossed her forearms and once again stuck out her pink tongue, now the new universal NewTimes teen sign for information-junk. Rob awkwardly replied, using instead two outstretched index fingers, while Frann in like-minded agreement extended a finger into his throat and graphically mimicked gagging.

This moment proved another telling one for Rob. For some reason, he hadn't mirrored Andry's outstretched tongue. This time there was something outrageously *erotic* about her gesture that would have been even more so had he returned it in like kind, so he substituted a less, in his mind, charged gesture, one sufficiently ample to remain one with his mob as well as collusively "partner" with Andry, which in fact, he desperately wanted to do. Frann and the remaining members of the group remained thankfully oblivious to Brie's inner struggle, but the memory of the moment alongside the previous one during which Jan had expressly presented both her naked tongue and body to him—*Hey, nakedness is nothing really, so how could it actually been 'just for him?'* his agile mind interjected—would together exert an even stronger grip on his every spare thought. Unfortunately, all the education concerning NewAmerican technology did little to thwart or redirect this uncomfortable introspection.

In overview, Rob/Brie led his mob, individually and collectively, to come to the general shared conclusion that the NewTimes held intriguing amenities that made living exclusively on NewTerra, if one could but afford it, worth the exceptional effort required. Successful mobs, he'd observed, craving these amenities, knowing full well that each and every one had been specifically engineered to be obsessive, addictive, and as wildly and crazily hedonistic as the era, organized themselves around ways of obtaining them. What continued to bother Brie, however, was that he, Andry and Frann clearly knew this, but Andry didn't seem to care in the least.

Chapter 10

As might be expected, NewTime youths like Brie, as they approached peak adolescence, would become increasingly adept and enamored with acronyms to the point that any conversation would often be carried out entirely in the latest ones, typically in coordination with body movements associated with whatever T-rips the conversing persons were experiencing. If proven useful, someone, somewhere, would inevitably take up the acronymic names of whatever was being expressed and string them together in a new way, creating a macro-acronym representing the information it encapsulated. If lucky, a good macro-acronym creator and marketer—in NewSpeak, an acronymeur— might see his or her creation spread from mob to mob in ever increasing waves, eventually working its way through the population of NewTerra and, when a critical planetary mass picked it up and began using it in common speech, throughout the entirety of colonized space. The more popular macro-acronymeurs would copyright and then register their new creations in the nearest governmental linguistic archives for acronymeurs files—LAFs for short—where enduring LAFs would eventually be branded and in exceptional instances massaged to contain some anagram of the inventor's name.

Jan—actually Simi Andry Jan [Jan-Rho], who, when first introduced, Brie had taken to first calling Jan, later Andry based on their mob association, and more recently Simi based on a (hopefully from Draff/Rob/Brie's perspective) increasingly intimate "friendship" if that was indeed where it was going—made her living as a professional acronymeur. Unknown at this time to either of the two, over her lifetime she would create and establish over two thousand popular enduring macro-acronyms, a hundred of which would end up being registered with and eventually acquired by one or more planetary governments to in due course be listed in the NewAmerican/NewTerran Linguistic Dictionary as being of special socio-economic significance. Each of these copyrighted, registered acronyms, whenever it was invoked in conversation and digitally recorded on one of the trillions of ever-watchful government cameras located seemingly everywhere, resulted in her being paid a use-royalty. Individually small, these royalties collectively produced enough sally to make her life on NewTerra both comfortable and, to the many who knew of her in this particular way, envious.

One particular coming-of-age amenity to which all youth, including Brie—Draff Rob Brie [Septican-Smite] to be more precise; now Draff to Simi—looked forward was Transitional Adaptive Reconstructive Surgery, or TARS. An extension of pre-Jacksonian skin art, it was an offshoot of tatooing, piercing and later, plastic surgery that allowed one to choose and obtain sophisticated body alterations or additions. TARS quickly became, like other new social technologies, the rage. It's initial expense made it a mark of the *nouveau riche,* like Simi, who had already begun making her fortune on an unfolding social technology. This, of course, drove the new technology to become ever more desired and widespread. Given the immense advancements in biological and medical sciences, there were no significant side effects to TARS. Not anymore at least, except for an instant rise in social status when the TARS was coupled with the acquisition of an official adult identity, or AID.

Brie's TARS-AID, as youth of his age had taken to calling it, would be a prehensile tail. By his reckoning, the extra appendage would come in handy whenever he needed a fifth hand, and, theoretically at least, it could also add a certain flair to pair coupling. His tail would be distinctly simian, an inch in diameter at its base and about four feet long, tapering to a fleshy point at the end, something he hoped his future intimates (like Simi?) would come to appreciate and enjoy. As he described it, his tail would be covered with a light dust of reddish-brown fur to make its whole length both comfortable and natural-appearing, while at the same time serving as an extra, exquisitely sensitive tactile appendage. The process of deciding, planning, paying for, registering, announcing, and finally having the TARS done honored another of the increasing many emerging NewTime societal rites of passage from adolescence into adulthood. More importantly, his prehensile tail would eventually provide Brie the single most important attribute of an AID of NewAmerica: a unique personal Biobrand.

Chapter 11

During the last week of formal holographic classes, it became Brie's time for another right of passage: memory buttressing, or as his mob liked to call it, Mind-Butting. For the next hour or so, his head would be encased in a large, white, hat-like apparatus provided to all adult learners by the government. During Mind-Butting, he would literally dream while awake, reliving his collective years of holographic lessons, re-ordering and re-associating them, moving the gist of what he'd heard and learned from longterm into permanent memory without conscious effort. Staring out an open window during the session with a combination of youthful impatience and outright adolescent envy at the world outside, it was as if he were simultaneously present in two different but overlapping worlds, the additional one constantly yet gently tucking away everything pertinent that his mind could extract from what he'd learned into his semi-consciousness permanent memory while consciously thinking about what he was seeing out the window.

Outside the window, two birds chirped and a puff of

wind rustled some nearby tree leaves.

Inside his head, Brie could sense the abstract litany of instruction in the voices of his holo-instructors replaying: "NewAmericans' physical condition, nutrition and general health have become nearly ideal, leaving biodiversity to whims of individual desire, epigenes and occasional serendipitously acquired thought-treasures—threasures. 'Poor' no longer related solely to money, but became based on one's unique combination of TARS-AID, sally, contro, education, threasures, curiosity, social effectiveness in work and overall consciousness."

Brie smiled. He preferred to think in terms of each person's "Designer Jeans"—DigJees he referred to them one day to Simi's delight and profit—the acronym under her expert hand immediately spreading like wildfire throughout their community and NewAmerica.

"DigJees," Brie said aloud, smiling at the multi-level pun that existed somewhere between real and alternate reality, somewhere between the room where he was still looking out of a window, and the one where his instructors' voices continued fast-forwarding, attempting to impress its content ever firmer in his mind. The incorporeal voices inside his head soon took on tonal variations of Brie's own voice revisiting, amending, restating everything had been previously stated: ContraSpray. Eugitors. CandyShades.

CandyCable. Forty-Seven Suits. TARS-AID. Mind-Butting. DigJees. New applications of existing technologies, and a myriad of new underpinnings for ever more novel theoretical technological concepts that would continue to fuel NewTerra's economic expansion, at the same time providing the glue necessary to bind together NewTerra's peoples.

About the middle of the Mind-Butt, a profound silence occurred outside the open window coupled with the scent of chlorine-fresh air and...*What is that other smell?* his mind asked, immediately replying, *Your own acrid sweat,* leading him to think further, *This Mind-Butt must be unusually intense.* "Draff to Simi! Draff to Billie and Simi!" his mouth wanted to say, but his mind couldn't get past repeating the thought without any physical manifestation.

In the meantime, the re-arranged and re-assembled voice of history inside his brain continued fast-forwarding on: "Innovation in quantum transport or QTrans... simultaneous appearance of one perfect, but mirror image copy of an object in another location...transport anything that could fit in the palm of a hand, anywhere in the universe if one but knew all four-dimensional target coordinates in time-space..." The key was, Brie knew, at the precise, carefully calculated position and moment, to break the quantum entanglement of the two objects, causing either the original or its perfect mirror-image copy to remain in existence. One or the other, but, of course, never both.

Using this technology, people began instantly translocating small objects over vast distances—things like small packets of nutrient water, and small consumer devices, but not living things. *Never* living things. Living things are primarily based on left-sided (L-) biochemicals, and changing them to right-sided (R-) biochemicals would inactivate many, leading to instant death. On the other hand, if an object was contaminated with a viral or, heaven forbid, a prion hitchhiker—nonliving outside of a biological host, they could be translocated upon or within the object— theoretically spreading illness or disease at the receiving end. With all brand new technologies like QTrans, there were always side effects to consider and be slowly worked out.

QTrans is all good and great, Brie thought in passing, *as long as whoever was behind the transport was willing to dispose of the still not-so-occasional transport aberration mess.* These days, every Fast Eddy on Terra was actively competing—meaning attempting to steal QTrans technology from the many closed, secretive, high-security corporate research laboratories—in order to sell to what they could uncover to whichever other corporation had the necessary contra to purchase the information and the practical ability to string it together into a patentable retail transportation system. Interestingly, in pure anticipation, the acronym for a system that *could* transport living things, especially humans—SuperQTrans—had already been invented, copyrighted, registered and was being actively introduced and promoted worldwide, though as yet, it represented an applied technology that had yet to materialize, the royalties for its use similarly. Everyone in the universe, including Brie, was holding his or her breath in anticipation of the expected any-day breakthrough announcement.

Outside the window, a momentary flash of light caught his attention. At least, he thought it a flash of light. *What was that?* Brie's conscious mind asked out of pure curiosity.

The sun glinting off something, another part of Brie's conscious mind replied, while the instructors' reconstituted information continued burrowing ever deeper into his head. It was interesting that the Mind-Butt continued droning on, oblivious to the flash or his awareness of it, if, in fact, there'd actually been a flash.

"...Legendary President Jackson's insightful paradigm shift..." a teacher's voice now sounding amazingly similar to his own continued in parallel.

The flash, if it had indeed happened, reminded him of a ray of bright sunlight reflecting off the curve of a polished chrome hood ornament of a car in a museum to which one of their holo-instructors had taken Brie's education group several years back. *Odd*, he caught himself thinking on what seemed an entirely different plane, *what tricks one's mind plays during a Mind-Butt.*

The re-processed voice continued recounting how wheeled internal combustion devices, the gas and petroleum industry, and the era's petrodollar economy the infamous President Brown had tried to elevate and control had vanished when juxtaposed against Jackson's future vision. Cars quickly became historical relics, pointed at and laughed about when one ran across one in a museum that would even waste the space displaying it. Anyone in Rob's educational group, if asked about Awheels, would shrug their shoulders and shake their heads in derision, then quickly change the subject to one of more contemporary interest. BWheels, for example. Formerly "bicycles," these contemporary multi-tasking, solar-powered BWheels now flourished, and possessing the most outrageously equipped ones had become the latest fad.

Brie's train of thought was forcibly dragged back to a previous week's lesson relating to cars: "With the demise of Awheels, roads were converted into wide BWheel pathways with large open walkways on either side."

An image of a converted roadway appeared as if

QTrans'ed into Brie's mind and began flickering like an ancient celluloid movie back to a walk he'd taken several days ago with his mob. Walking these days was tantamount to taking a personal vacation, though in most of his mob's minds, it was a rather humdrum one given the government's obsession with requiring walkers to help with returning everything surrounding the walkway back to its "cultivated natural" state.

"Cultivated Natural," the voice inside his head echoed.

Cultivated natural state, thought Brie, his eyes drooping, his head nodding sleepily. *What left in this universe was truly 'natural'? Or, for that matter, what could be 'cultivated natural'? The only thing* really *natural to him these days was his mob, and it was highly questionable how truly natural any mob actually was. No, not mobs. His memories—which are right now in the process of being Mind-Butted...Oops!* Draff Rob Brie [Septican-Smite] lazily raised an arm to brush away a fly that appeared to be buzzing around his ear.

Is this a real fly? he wondered, smelling nothing.

"Draff to Billie and Simi. Draff to Simi. Draff...to..." his drooling lips struggled to say.

"Simi to Draff," came a distant, ethereal answer, but whether real or a figment of his desperate imagination, he couldn't tell.

Reawakening to Simi's giggles and Billie's chortles, Draff found his two favorite nest mates staring at him from either side. The fly had been holographically engineered by Billie and projected against Draff's ear replete with buzzing sound and projected sensation.

"For Jackson's sake! Pay attention!" played from somewhere in the middle of Draff/Rob/Brie's head alongside the vague memory-image of an all too familiar holo-instructor yelling at him, the memory-image reconstituting and re-inserting itself into a semi-conscious mental dialog within a hail of Billie's guffaws.

"For Jackson's sake! pay attention, Draff!" Billie Frann Frunk [Tordon-Cass] mimicked, invoking Brie's physically-intimate first name while taking a swing at Draff's white-turbaned head. "Yes. For Jackson's sake!" Simi echoed, her ingratiating voice conveying, as always, substantively more...at least that's how it seemed to Draff/Rob/Brie's confused mind.

Draff reflexively ducked from what turned out to be a holographic swing of Billie's arm. That same moment Billie laughed loudly, Simi smiled coyly, and the two vanished, leaving him once again alone in the room staring out the window, the device covering his head exerting itself less subtly this time: "Then came Great Ambient Paradox— GAP—sudden 'in-everyone's-face' results of years of environmental disregard during the late Total Meltdown. Urbanites turned to living in higher and higher structures to locate themselves above ever thickening, ever expanding pollution. Suburban businesses did exactly opposite, locating themselves ever deeper in an increasingly waste-filled ocean. The land in-between—the surface of what would become NewTerra—became so unlivable it had to initially be abandoned. All this resulted from people's desperate focus at that time on securing enough sally or contro to simply survive. Once Jackson's government awakened fully to NewTerra's plight and addressed GAP-festering, heavily industrialized landscapes, things began slowly reverting, but in a distinctly re-humanized manner."

Re-humanized? Really? Brie caught himself thinking. *An odd term, 're-humanized'.* It had been, in his opinion, much more than that!

"Encouraged by their government, NewAmericans slowly began to re-define what recreation meant. It soon became 'in' to take one hour or even one or more days off work to tour formerly ravaged byways, officially renaming in the vernacular the animals and plants they noted while walking or Bwheeling.

Naming the animals and plants after themselves...?

"The idea was to inspire feelings of environmental stewardship through government established and funded official Naming Ceremonies—N-Cares—whereby human caretakers and the animal or plant names of their now 'cultivated natural' darlings would be publicly announced, ceremoniously celebrated, then recorded digitally in ever-expanding governmental N-Cares information vaults called I-Cares."

The honor caught on and the practical result was immediate: I-Cares, in essence governmental genetic diversity repositories, sprang up everywhere, and awardees gladly paid for public recognition, contractually committing themselves to husbanding the animals or plants which they had name-recognized for the duration of the human's life. As a further honorific, caretakers were permitted to wear a light blue colored armband. At the same time, the government inserted a tiny, inert, bioluminescent DNA tag into the now protected entity, identifying it as under the care and protection of the government by way of that particular human caretaker.

"This program singularly changed the surface of NewAmerica into one citizen-tended, cultivated-natural paradise."

To this, Brie's now lolling mind added, *and many were becoming so enamored with the program, it began taking on the attributes of a 'culturally natural' religion.* This was, of course, much to the chagrin of youth who, like Brie's mob, often joked about it as being a personal challenge to "Keep ON the Grass."

"Like other social technologies," the voice inside his head continued, "NewAmerica's wholesale return to nature—no matter how artificially contrived—encouraged people to indulge themselves in a second highly addictive and surprisingly healthful activity: physical exercise. This became of even greater import as an increasing portion of people prepared to spend the remainder of their lives outside NewTerran gravity."

It was an established fact that, outside of Mother Earth's gravity, human and animal skeletal systems, even plant stem systems, rapidly adapted, making return to full gravity risky, and, once the organism was fully off-world adapted, potentially fatal. This proved especially so if the individual had been gestated, born and/or raised as an infant outside Mother Earth's gravity. The only preventative was vigorous physical exercise against the equivalent of one earth's gravity. As a consequence, NewTerrans were coming to appreciate the importance of exercise as a key factor in maintaining choice, longevity and quality of life. In summary, people—NewTerrans especially—slowly b e g a n returning to the ancient Greek ideal of naked beauty.

Brie, Fran, and Jan, core nest mates together if only holographically, knew full well what that meant. Each knew that a whole new world awaited their transition to adulthood, an alluring world full of nearly unimaginable delights alongside immense attendant responsibilities. They had only to survive, hopefully in optimal shape, in NewAmerica and on NewTerra long enough to make their choice and claim their birthright. With that thought, Brie, together with the holographic images of Billie and Simi, reached up, grabbed the large turban-like Mind-Butt headpiece and tossed it aside—meaning, of course, that Draff/Rob/Brie tossed it aside with the other two's encouragement. The fact that it responded to their collective half-real, half-projected actions was a mark in Brie's mind that the Mind-Butt had basically come to its end, anyway.

Brie shook his head to clear it for the day ahead, and what happened next would be indelibly imprinted in his adolescent memory more powerfully than any Mind-Butt could ever have accomplished: He noticed as he deep breathed, the flicker of a bare arm flash momentarily on either side of him. One was clearly Billie's and the other Simi's. Each placed a holographic hand on one of his shoulders, and together the two gently, lovingly, visually, stroked Draff's bare arm.

There was, however, a surprising difference between his two friends' actions. While Draff could well *imagine* the feel of Billie's strong hand on his arm, he could swear he actually *felt* Simi's delicate fingers stroke his flesh.

How can that be? he wondered in surprise, the hairs on his forearms rising. *How did she do that?*

To the best of Draff's knowledge, no one had yet figured out a way to make projected holograms actually *feel* corporeal. to another He had, therefore, decided that it must be his imagination, heightened by the confusion in his mind at having just completed the Mind-Butt, when he noticed the familiar spiciness of Simi's smell, richer, more complex and inviting than he had ever noticed before. It lingered in the air where her fingers a moment ago had been, while the images of Billie and Simi, both naked as when born, standing at his either side, remained: Billie with a childishly innocent, adoring smile on his face; Simi staring intensely into Draff's eyes with her haunting half-knowing, half-questioning smile.

Raymond Gaynor

Chapter 12

It is necessary to pause here in order to point out several important prior assumptions that all NewAmericans now hold in common: First, youth during this era, like Draff Rob Brie, Billie Frann Frunk and Simi Andry Jan were accustomed to constant close social contact, though, physically, they lived largely solitary lives. The nearest analog during pre-Jacksonian times would be youths of that time who grew up socializing on cellular phones while shyly avoiding face-to-face contact. It wasn't uncommon back then to see two individuals standing next to each other, communicating solely through their phones. Holographic socialization, however, exponentially upped the feeling of adolescent awkwardness should any youths actually meet in person.

Second, eons of open promiscuity prior to Jacksonian times during which coupling was inevitably accompanied by the fear of death from acquired sexually-transmitted diseases, had returned in the older adult population with the flowering of social technologies.

Third, the world, whether at the mob, group, community, nation, planetary or colonial system level was controlled, as in the ancient days, more by rash youth than the wise and aged. Quite frankly, the aged had other interests and a myriad of things to accomplish before departing this world. It wasn't that youth were interested or skilled in politics and government (though the *best* of youth, like Brie, Frunk and Jan were certainly heavily inculcated in these from the earliest possible age). For most governing was one of their responsibilities by default. The founder and first president of NewAmerica, President Jackson, had foreseen the necessity of downplaying this in order to discourage citizen anarchy, and had, from the first, incorporated the idea of youthful leadership into the NewAmerica's psyche.

Finally, "nations" like NewAmerica barely fit the pre-meltdown definition of such. It would be more accurate to speak of communities, and communities of communities, rather than nations *per se*. Socio-economically, communities, at one moment cooperated with and the next competed with other communities, determining the overall tenor of NewAmerica, and, by default, NewTerra, and, because of NewTerra's pivotal role in the socio-economic fabric of the times, all of humanity spread throughout the universe. Pre-meltdown nations had been subject to constant warfare, being fought over by politicians attempting to subtly or forcibly espouse their particular beliefs on other landed or more privileged populations. By the time of the meltdown, nations had already become anachronisms, largely ignored by youth who slowly, operationally redefined them as communities based largely on social similarities and differences.

Rob, in the very bud of youth at twenty years of age, repositioned his tail against the floor for added balance. He liked what he saw reflected in the 3-D wall mirror. Turning his virile, nude body from side-to-side he examined his projection, musing on all that had happened since he, Frann and Andry had raised their arms towards each other in their pledge of mob fealty more than ten years ago.

Rob smiled, recalling the moment with particular pleasure, and allowed the feeling to course through him, however quickly it dissipated. What was and had been were both interesting, but all this musing wasn't going to get him anywhere, and getting somewhere—anywhere—was what life was all about at his age. Two questions in particular were nagging at him today: Where exactly today's "somewhere" was, and what, if anything, he should wear to get there faster and more boldly.

Clothes? Jackson, now there was an interesting anachronism. Until one completed TARS, and registered and accepted one's AID, clothes were strongly frowned upon though in some distinctly retro circles still tolerated, but with general public disgust and distrust. After TARS-AID, adult clothing was even *more strongly* discouraged, being outright prohibited in all public and many private spaces. The contemporary drift was that the absence of clothing imparted a feeling of security to passersby, given that nakedness was a way of demonstrating that one was completely weaponless and need not be feared. It also allowed bodies to more clearly broadcast and receive emotional signals of interest and intention. Wearing clothes during the immediate post-Jacksonian period, had been a forefront issue requiring decisive, contentious legislative action.

Only Enforcers these days always wore clothes, and that was primarily to broadcast their authoritative status and, of course, to intimidate. For adults, aside from broadcasting they were social outliers or intentional misfits, clothes continued to serve primarily as a way to advertise one's work—one's brand—one's con for short—as well as individual propensities or strengths—one's pros. At some point during each person's SweetSixteen, that singularly important official transition from child to adulthood, he or she would end up declaring their pros and principal con. During that crucial period was also when one would end up determining if and what clothes he or she would wear. "One person—one con—one clothes," was the residual government line.

At some point during the pivotal SweetSixteen year, each adolescent turning adult was required to formally record his or her pros on an official government billet list in the local archives. Replacing the now extinct debutante balls, this practice became known as "playing-D-Ball." In practical terms, that meant having to choose from available government-approved cons based not only on one's individual pros and *desired* con, but based on society's needs as well. For most, that meant selecting the one available con that best applied, and accepting it's attending billet from among the few available or the least heavily wait-listed.

But back to clothes. At this moment, Rob was definitely feeling more Robbish than Draffish, having come to terms in late adolescence with being somewhat of an outlier given his unique gifts and talents. Given his pros, the only real "fit" for him in terms of available con billets ended up being "undifferentiated, short-term, sexual entertainer and companion." The only real "fit" in terms of clothes, if any, would therefore be a high drain, custom-made Eugitor Forty-Seven ShimmerSuit (with his already accumulated contro, with optional convenience slits that changed color based on body temperature and pheromone secretion). In other words, absolutely minimal outward clothing that matched and broadcast his moment-to-moment feelings. For his con, this billet's attendant "clothing" requirement was the current "in" thing among rebellious young adults. In fact, he didn't really need a ShimmerSuit to broadcast his moment-to-moment physical inclinations at all, given that his newly acquired tail, simply by its positions and flick-movements broadcast them well enough to observant onlookers. The tail repeatedly proved this when he was among potentially intimate clients. On the other hand, perhaps because of his innate differences and the tail, he'd begun once again succumbing to the fear of being *recognized* as different, and paradoxically now felt the urge for some kind of covering that would provide a certain amount of anonymity and protection when he was out and about, on his way to work, or when plying his con among strangers.

Minutes later, resolving in his mind to cover himself, but, in the spirit of the billet, minimalistically when actually "in con," he slipped into, then stood back to dreamily admired the projected reflection of himself this time encased in a custom-made ShimmerSuit that at least presented his tail unclothed. Smiling at the sight of his reflexively flicking tail, his thoughts snapped back to his SweetSixteen. He had, with the help of his current custodian, identified his pros, selected a con and billet, declined Body Cellular Memory Cleansing—BCMC—a no-cost erasure by governmental specialists of all noncritical pre- and mid-adolescent body cell memories, thereby resetting body cell age to that of early childhood, theoretically adding another decade to his physical life. The fact was, he didn't need it, having attained a level of consciousness far in excess of others his physical age. His SweetSixteen "coming out" plan was now officially recorded in the Emory-Shi Public Hall of Records as part of his coming-of-age. He could, of course, edit it anytime before his actual SweetSixteen, though only at substantial draw.

In Rob's case—he would be Rob, he decided, to his customers—he was immediately recruited by and subsequently began regularly conning in his chosen billet at Slams, a private club that offered proprietary T-rips in drinkable, chewable or skin-absorbable form at exorbitant draw. At Slams, clients could, for outrageous additional draw, don one of the club's proprietary Eugitor FortySeven suits for the enhanced sensual or sexual experience of his or her life. So suited, a client could enjoy the experience either from his gender perspective, an opposite gender perspective, Draff's perspective, or, for even more contro, any combination, either in realtime (popular with the young) or savetime (popular with the older, "souvenir" set).

Unknown to Slams' clients, however, the club units were not *entirely* virtually true-to-life. Slams' units secretly included several hidden safety programs that would instantly kick in to moderate the client's experience, if, for example, Draff's physical response to a client were either less than ideal or overmuch. To Draff's clients, the idea of getting into another's body during a period of physical intimacy was such a turn-on that a good many of Slams clients availed themselves of this additional draw option, which, of course, made Slams, and thereby Rob, both imminently successful *and* rich, while giving the club an appropriately sleazy yet high-quality sophistication, as well as an alluring reputation of sensual and sexual intrigue. For the most part, Draff preferred working with natural genetic females with all-female working parts, but he wasn't adverse to others. He simply preferred the former, always providing an exceptional bang for the client's contro and physical buck.

As it turned out, Draff Rob Brie [Septican-Smite], as Rob, came to quickly love what he did. His billet was perfectly suited to his innate pro's, especially his curiosity and individual predilections, and because of the unusually good match, his PNI or Public Notoriety Index always ran high. Everyone who was anyone quickly came to know him or at least of him. They had to if they wanted to remain socially "in." It was part of the whole NewTimes game.

As a consequence, to protect himself in public, Rob soon had to take to wearing high-draw flack when traveling between home and workplace, and *his* was nothing less than the finest. Not only could it ward off assaultive individuals, projections, programs and most weaponry, but it adapted itself exquisitely to whatever he chose to wear, even the thin molecular covering of his custom ShimmerSuit. Flack like his was still relatively new, making him of even more public interest.

Visually, Rob's flack worked by molecularly liquefying and visually diffusing upon any sudden attempted intrusion, first confusing any would-be assailant as to exactly what and where the intended target was, and second, crystalizing and absorbing the impact of any intrusive instrument or program. The impact of a bullet from an illegal vintage handgun—all devices that projected lethal objects had been outlawed planet-wide for years—or the point of a sharp blade would be completely assimilated, leaving the entire unit stronger and even more resilient before returning to normal. Even so, a very slowly moving hand, for example, could be permitted by him to slip through, allowing those he desired to experience flesh-to-flesh contact. This latter innovation was beyond state-of-the-art, and proved wonderfully amusing and incredibly popular at club parties. It was also an outstanding marketing device, which Rob never hesitated to use when introducing himself to new clients, especially ultra-rich ones.

Flacked and suited, Rob was always ready and eager for another day's action at Slams. In truth, the hardest part of the day was getting there. Slams was an easy, across-town jaunt from where he lived, but in urban NewAmerica, that meant navigating through several million people. For most urban pedestrians, it required the daily ritual of checking where the largest crowds were and avoiding them while slowly working one's way towards the destination. For the increasingly infamous Draff Rob Brie, any path was a minefield of admirers, sycophants, hustlers and criminals, all well aware of his sally, draw and contro value.

Rob sighed and touched the inside of his wrist to switch on his Integrated Global Position System transponder, Auditory Directional Advisor, Voice Recorder and direct realtime communication line to the local enforcement agency. Should something untoward happen along the way he at least wouldn't be alone. All NewTerra would instantly know. He paused in the doorway to give some last-minute instructions to his home privacy system and sauntered through the pre-programmed, one-way, tensor-liquid door. *Easy to leave—difficult to return. A lot like life*, Rob thought.

The nine hundredth floor on which he lived was dimly lit, silent, and at first glance, appeared deserted. He walked quickly to the lift, cautiously scanning the hallways for any signs of life—*for my con, the greatest danger is always another human*, he reflected, passing his palm briefly in front of the elevator call plate just slow enough for it to recognize and record his wrist biometrics.

Rob ascribed to the belief that given its complexity and diversity, the multiverse couldn't be populated just with humans, and that whatever other life forms there were would likely (or at least hopefully) have evolved well beyond humankind, given the short time *Homo sapiens* had been around to evolve.

And in even shorter time they would have begun to evolve sexually, his overactive mind added in repost, *so the act of coupling should become increasingly pleasant and less violent in the future.* That, of course, went solidly against most NewTerrans' experience, where for millenia the close correspondence between sex and violence had both physically and emotionally *increased* while, paradoxically, the legal and to some extent public social acceptance of the two in general had only titularly decreased.

What would my con be like in another universe? his curious inner voice asked, trailing off as the lift door hissed open and a disembodied but tantalizingly familiar feminine voice invited him to carefully step in. It took him a few moments to recognize the familiar voice without a smell. It was Simi's. The lift had processed his wrist biometrics and, correctly identifying him, his current partner and his current mood, adjusted it's humanized voice interface to one that would make his journey down the hundreds of floors more comforting.

Interesting, Rob thought as the elevator silently descended, a popular tune playing barely perceptibly in the background, the singer's voice once again Simi's. Rob smiled and his molecular suit warmed slightly, the almost but not quite entirely hidden inner areas of its various normally dull, metal-grey gill-like slits developing a soft, fleshy glow. *Why are all the environmental sensors about me focused today on Simi?* he wondered, smiling again, his full lips abruptly twisting into a reactive grimace. There was something actually disquieting about today. He should be more cautious, but instead, a sense of adventurous recklessness was filling his mind as the elevator continued its swift down, down, downward course.

Well, reckless it is then, he thought as the lift door hissed open and the unit instructed him to carefully step out, yet again in Simi Andry Jan's inviting voice.

Chapter 13

As a result of his unique education, Rob had acquired the equivalent of a *de novo* master's degree in astronautics, yet he fancied himself more a student of emotional history, receiving particular enjoyment from stockpiling knowledge about people's reactions to NewTerra and NewAmerica's pasts. Of all the historical tidbits he'd acquired over the years, he prided himself most on his collective emotional history about the little-recognized, even less acknowledged Trauma-Affective Revolution which had, by his reckoning, begun well before Jackson, Tripler, Clarke and Stewart had had to face the overwhelming societal trauma of the Total Meltdown of the then United States of America. The result of his investigations appeared on a lesser-known organizational blog, the report referred to by the few affectionados in his field as The Brie TAR-Paper. As its acronym implied, this "revolution" was not so much in response to the series of technological innovations as it was an *emotional-ideological* change in thinking and acting quite as powerful and all-encompassing as any other revolution. But even that didn't do justice to the profound depth of the effect that TAR would ultimately have, again in his mind, on his and subsequent generations.

It would be more accurate to say TAR was more of an awakening in individual consciousness. A fork in the road of mental evolution that had up to this point favored the most willingly and capably physically violent. It was an awakening leading to an entirely new viewpoint regarding the very reason for human existence: why, for example, some humans—and that certainly included his mob, or more precisely he, Billie and Simi—had actually *had* to be present at this particular place at this particular time in order to sustain the awakening. Yet it was much, much more than that. It was an emotional-ideological revolution—a complete change not only in the way any one human thought, but the way he or she assigned meaning to what was happening. Most importantly, it represented a collective change in how one *felt* about it all. In his mind, it was the start of a second evolutionary pathway that would ultimately doom *Homo sapiens* to extinction, and usher in the next humanoid species. And it would happen within his lifetime before his and his mob's open eyes.

He knew—he could intrinsically *feel*—the paradigm shift had already begun within himself and his mob, and as a consequence, his group, community, NewAmerica and

NewTerra. And it was happening almost entirely beneath academic, public and even governmental recognition, though it was, in his opinion, the single most important event that had occurred or perhaps would ever occur in NewAmerica since it's rise from the ashes of the former United States of America.

Dodging into a unoccupied alcove in an otherwise unbroken, infinitely long concrete wall that defined the right side of the urban walkway before him, Rob stretched his muscles, then, with a flash of his wrist, paid a machine embedded in the alcove to pour him a steaming cup of Azuki, the newest substitute for one of the last holdovers from the "old days:" coffee. Real coffee was no more. Outlawed by the government when the potent brew of addictive stimulants and co-carcinogens came to finally be acknowledged as such, the government, though not necessarily the populace, reluctantly let go of it. He swirled the dark brown liquid, held in the fifteen-minute long, transparent magnetic induction "cup" in his hands, breathing in its rich, pungent, bittersweet aroma. The aroma was so pungent, it caused him to momentarily reel; his heightened sense of smell having increased as he matured.

Human history was littered with trauma and its companion psychological violation. The two were used by occasional well-meaning but basically ignorant or blatantly criminal political, social, educational, military and business leaders as well as myriads of not-so-well-meaning holdovers from the days of Brown's administration. Sadly, the two found widespread application during the meltdown by individuals quite willing to ignore the fact that the use of violence, in the end, simply fueled and secured its further propagation. Some, Rob included, held that it resulted in a "voracious circle"—a swirling vortex that held humanity in unrelenting thrall, seemingly forever inhibiting humanity from moving on from its painful cultural adolescence into more pleasant maturity.

Rob took another pull of the rich drink and shook his head. It was hard to understand why people for so many millennia were not able to grasp the basic principal that trying to change things using violence—trying to eradicate trauma with more trauma—just didn't work. Civilization after civilization—generation after generation—had meticulously recorded this mistake for the next civilization or generation to learn, but always without success. Even now, he wasn't sure humanity, hovering on the cusp of a new consciousness, was, as a whole, actually "getting it."

Early twenty-first century psychologists had begun to uncover bits and pieces of tantalizing information suggesting there did, indeed, exist an alternative to violence and violation. A way to not only replace this old thinking, but maybe even erase both the current and resistant past effects of trauma, but attempts to apply this information fell short. Serially referred to as "*gestalt,*" holistic, and affective approaches, adherents—then called therapists—in an effort to bring together and generalize the process, had begun to create non-traditional consensus-building, cooperative, affirmative, Rogerian, intercultural, and reconcilliative forms of communication—"peace negotiation"—when what they needed was an approach that specifically addressed the *effects* of what simply proved to be yet more coercive therapies. A few educators correctly intuited that this new construct needed to be curiosity-based, discovery-driven, enthusiasm-based and, most importantly, self-directed, claiming that contemporary "teaching" had become so corrupted—so traumatic—that students and teachers alike were falling prey to traumatic side effects, namely depression, burnout, loss of empathy—a surprisingly wide spectrum—that invariably ended in sociopathy.

At the same time, businesses all over NewTerra began succumbing to the seductive "for profit" ethic with its promise of increasingly "Faster" Eddie accumulation of wealth and power. No longer even attempting to conceal it's unbridled core of violence, this business approach was slated to eventually become a despised aphorism representing a license to fleece the "suckers" of the world.

"Take everything; give nothing back."

Luckily, this ruinously right-in-your-face "it's-okay-to-lie-cheat-and-steal-as-long-as-you-don't-get-caught" ethic was fleeting. Global disintegration and "businessification"—"giving everyone and everything the business" in PopSpeak—led a few outspoken individuals to boldly assert it all had to stop. What was needed, they said, was *service* over *product*, emphasizing human (as well as animal and later plant) enlightenment and self-actualization over the illusion of money, power and immortality.

The change, where it took hold, didn't happen quickly or easily. Despite the well planned, highly orchestrated, top-down restructuring of human society during Jacksonian times, it took a grass roots insurrection—a total rejection of pre-Jacksonian style business and its root concept of competitive violence to convince people that unconstrained greed and ever-increasing profit would *never* trickle wealth down to the masses. The justification for change was the ineffectiveness of business to address the infrastructure deficiencies that began emerging *en masse* during the Total Meltdown.

It proved a singular time in history for education, during which students—now called "learners"—LNRs—individually and collectively demanded that teachers stop teaching, and instead provide learning resources and demonstrate their use, encouraging LNRs to unlock their own latent creativity and apply critical thinking to their enlightened discoveries—the very abilities that their former teachers purported yet so miserably failed to implement. In the process, non-traumatic learning was "rediscovered."

With the collapse of teaching in favor of learning, another shift occurred among LNRs: that of valuing cooperative-group over competitive-individual learning. This new educational perspective was the one within which Rob and mob had received their education.

While many considered these changes in education to be yet another of the many innovations introduced by President Jackson, "teaching" had already begun to walk the path of extinction well before, during a nationwide Brownian rave-wave of privatization. But not just privatization, but privatization reflecting Brown's form of ultra-competitive, and, by nature, ultra-violent form of ultra-Capitalism—first within business, then medicine, then education, then government, then politics, then social institutions. The horror of it all only surfaced into public awareness when business began arrogantly and irresponsibly utilizing marketing and advertising techniques incorporating propaganda to maximize sales of less desirable products by eliminating the most desirable. What inevitably followed was an absence of outstanding products and services resulting in the need for consumers to pay additionally for anything they actually wanted, spurring a wave of unrelenting "inflation" that further concentrated wealth and control in the hands of the richest, most ruthless and sadly, incompetent.

Applying the principals of UltraCap consistently resulted in the appearance of a myriad of new "styles" of products, each relying on popularity as a measure of value, that is, "branding" as the sole trustworthy measure of quality. while obfuscating any objective information that might otherwise influence the consumer. Food, for example, was no longer accompanied by any data regarding chemicals used in its growing or preparation. Initially, it seemed to work, though, in the end consumers came to realize that they could not trust corporations hell-bent on showing increasing profit to provide *safe* food, only food that sold well. In this world of increasingly inhuman executives, controlling ever more increasing-for-profit corporations, offering ever more useless, inappropriate, undesirable, and, in the end *unsafe* products, in Rob's mind, was not just President Brown's Achilles' Heel, but more appropriately his Achilles' Hell, ultimately causing the man's downfall and bringing about the Total Meltdown.

At the time, of course, it hadn't seemed a big deal. People—especially those known as "influencers"—easily succumbed to the promise of ever increasing profit and their own soaring greed. The truth was, in those days, many private institutions soon had no goal other than to generate ever increasing profits, in the end, providing the people who were forced to provide these inferior products and services with little more than a slightly higher contro or sally, and, in the case of college and university graduates, often less than they had received before being "educated" and left in massive personal debt.

The inane leading the inane, increasing-for-profit businesses eventually began succumbing to their own clever, oblique advertising and marketing, believing their own propaganda, and, in the process, losing themselves, and what little remained of their humanity and their souls.

Business, Rob thought, *began serving itself rather than providing the increasingly needed products and services essential to satisfy humanity's real needs, wants and desires.* At least, that was how he saw it. Business during Brown's time as President had been hijacked.

During the Total Meltdown, the whole mess crumbled under the weight of the hidden behemoth: Defeat-filled citizens no longer able to discern the truth and make an informed decision, further opened the door to Total Meltdown. Few had predicted it, and none, not even the "left-leaning radicals"—LRads—appreciated the extent to which the businessification of America had turned people into consuming idiots.

Rob took a last draught of hot Azuki and shook the container in the air. It instantly disappeared and he peeked warily out of the alcove. *Life before Jackson*, he thought with disgust. Nowadays, businesses were barred from indulging in UltraCap. Furthermore, increasing demand for products and services by off-Terran travelers and emigrants during their long transits through interplanetary space fostered a new generation of Earth-based commerce, by law required to utilize consumer-safe, less-traumatic, cooperative, distance provisioning. Anything less could increase feelings isolation and confinement experienced by travelers and threaten the integrity of the entire space industry.

Most businesses still maintained an administrative presence, usually a small, palatial-appearing, typically underground, undersea or orbital room, for formal, ritualized, public-recognition events. For example, in education, the granting of school, college and university certificates and diplomas were held in resplendent, holographic, real or saved time and broadcast universe-wide.

Nowadays, faculty, instructors and vocational trainers worked holographically from their homes often asynchronously with LNRs located all over the populated universe. LNRs typically formed small cooperative learning groups, selecting and paying for a popular and institutionally unencumbered local mentor to further help them. Graduated LNRs who could demonstrate *how to apply* what they learned to "real life" were in far great demand over those simply sporting a certificate or diploma.

No longer slaves of physical institutions, faculty, instructors, vocational trainers and mentors were free to work with whichever LNRs chose them. In the end, the only requirements to receiving a certificate, diploma or degree were a reasonable knowledge of one's topic of interest, its social history, the knowledge to apply it—be it based on scientific-factual or human-opinion oriented evidence—the ability to think critically, and work cooperatively, displaying the wisdom to know how to responsibly apply they had learned.

Noticing a pair of Enforcers approaching, Rob pulled abruptly back into the alcove and thought of his own formal education. Thankfully, their learning experience had never been relegated to a Pre-Jacksonian "classroom," classrooms being, quite simply, too sterile, too resource-poor, too unimaginative, too controlling and, in being too controlling, too volitionally constraining (read "violent" in NewSpeak) to support the deeper kind of learning his mob craved and NewAmerica wanted its youth to learn. Everything a person experienced or accomplished inside and outside of formal education was considered a legitimate part of a LNRs education. Rob's astronautic degree had included hours and hours of holographic time on testbeds, trainers and simulators. He was not only a theoretical physicist and cosmologist, but an equally qualified engineer, and a licensed on-and- off-world pilot. In short, he, like so many of his colleagues was the best he or she was capable of being. The result was far beyond anything anyone in the past could ever have imagined.

The two Enforcers he'd noted paused and began talking together a short distance ahead in the direction he needed to go. Rob reflexively swept his hand in the air in front of his face to call heads up projections of his personal RSS feeds. Scanning them for what, if anything, might have caught the two Enforcer's attention, Rob had to acknowledge that he was these days, indeed, privileged. And privileged adults were dedicated, life-long LNRs of which Rob was no exception. He had, for example, already accumulated considerable learning hours towards additional master's degrees in sociology, psychology and performing arts simply from exercising his billet-con at Slams. Participation, including active, passive and "lurking" time in addition to experience counted towards his continuing education, and one of the perks of continued education was the numerous resulting feeds he was now scanning.

Rob smiled to himself. His current con was more like anal-lysis 101 really, given the physical demands of many of Slams' clients. *Jackson, I know that I know as much if not more sociology, psychology, and performing arts from working the sexual entertainment-and-escort industry than most clinical psychologists in practice.* He smiled again, remembering that his life experience creds and resulting degrees would continue to accumulate throughout his life, slowly changing his official pro and con profiles, affording him new opportunities to utilize and apply what he learned, enjoyed and did well at. *That was what education was ultimately supposed to be about anyway, wasn't it?* Rob thought to himself, his tail twitching as he returned to mulling over a question that had been nagging him since he'd left the nest earlier today: where *today's* "anywhere" would be and how to get there faster. So far, the RSS feeds had revealed no indication as to why, or if indeed the two chatting Enforcers might have been interested in him.

When the Enforcers stopped chatting and walked past him, Rob breathed out, yawned, and stretched until all the tension in his muscles eased. The suit immediately turned to a favorite metallic blue, complete with potential gill-like oral, axillary and combined crotch-and-anal slits. Clearly he was feeling safer and more relaxed than a few minutes ago when the Enforcers had paused nearby to talk. He wriggled within the suit until the sensors relocated their favorite spots, and, again waving a hand, projected a holographic heads up reflection of himself. Grinning at the iridescent blue aura glowing about him (undoubtedly the result of his recollection of last night with Simi), the air began vibrating with expectation. *Exactly how it was last night, and exactly the right presentation for today*, thought Draff/Rob, irrespective of where today's "anywhere" might happen to ultimately end up taking him. Noting the crisp, clean, almost tangy smell filling his space, he wove into the crowds walking to and fro on the pathway before him. Others might not notice the smell, but he did, and the smell matched his olfactory memory of last night. *Simi,* his mind whispered. *Simi is this moment's 'anywhere'.*

Rob moved forward down the corridor to another familiar location where he bolted through a liquid door into an open, languidly lit room with holographic projections of the earth beneath him, the sky above and open air on all sides. Peering at the eight hundred ninety-nine floors of building towering to his right and above, he paused to let his Integrated Global Position System Transponder update his location on the walkway, community, nation, planet, solar system and universe.

Something pleasant was tickling the back of his mind.

A memory. One he distinctly wanted to recall. Mentally recalling the holographic "heads up" display that was part of his unique shimmer-suit, a series of choices unavailable to most of the other inhabitants of NewTerra floated in the air immediately in front of him. Choosing one, he linked it mentally to the memory fragment, and projected a proxy-self to search his mind to locate and identify the fragment. Having done so, and realizing it was all about last night with Simi, he ordered his self-proxy to return to the floor high above where his day had originated. In his mind, the ghostly apparition of his proxy-self wafted noiselessly down the walkway into the elevator, and onto the floor back in space and time to that particular place last night. The outline of a liquid door glowed dimly. The pulsing warm glow, keyed by his Integrated Global Position System Transponder's signature meant she was looking forward to him joining her. Sending his proxy forward in front of the door just long enough for the doorway to recognize him, he projected himself to enter into the small chamber where he could barely discern the sound of Simi's gentle, slow, breathing. She was still sleeping after last night's debauch. And why not? He'd be in bed next to her right now if he didn't so enjoy slamming. Thinking of her, the edges of his suit's crotch began to thicken, glisten, and in the barely discernible inside of the slit, glow a faint pinkish hue, slowly turning to brilliant orange and finally deep, rich red. The same was true of his proxy, as he approached her in his proxy state. He'd have to be careful: Proxy or not, his suit's automatic response would broadcast his interest and prove sexually intriguing to any interested party on the walkway watching.

Groping about like a glowing ghost in the darkness, the proxy followed Simi's intoxicating scent. Breathing the scent in deeply, proxy-Draff and thereby Draff/Rob couldn't help but think about the delights he and Simi had shared *in persona* last night, when after evening nourishment, they had mutually entered on the other's digital life-record their night's consensual love-making interest. He watched as his proxy cuddled warmly into Simi's naked embrace, her scent driving him wild, his body screaming for sexual release. The thought caused his proxy-body to release a tsunami of male pheromones, causing any remaining barriers between them in the vision to melt away, as they had when they were physically together that night.

Chapter 14

Immersed in the memory, Draff/Rob relived the next morning, when he was making preparations to leave their nest for Slams, and drew in a deep breath through his quivering nostrils to reaffirm something he had always known but of which he had to regularly remind himself: *He was fundamentally different from others*. And in a freakish sort of way, made all the more so by the fact that his extraordinary sense of smell was a natural gift, not an ARS, and one of which he had been consciously aware since well before birth. Now a young adult, his consciousness seemed to be expanding at light speed, and it was *all linked to his sense of smell*. During early adolescence, his highly sensitive and discriminating sense of smell had come to seem quite normal to him, but, he reminded himself, it had taken him many years to realize that his idea of "normal" smell wasn't anywhere near normal.

He could recall at two years of age, holding food in front of his nose and smelling it before tasting. Not a big deal really, but unusual in that most children that age placed anything within grasp directly into their mouth. Yet it was unusual enough for other children, and sometimes even his companions, to eventually begin teasingly calling him a dog. Unbeknown to his serial custodians, his instructors, nest mates or other children, the attribution, when flippantly tossed his way hurt him deeply.

At three and four, while other kids were busy learning how to make friends with each other, Rob—he was, after all, Rob, not Brie or Draff to most back then—withdrew into himself. In truth, he never felt the need to see, talk, touch or interact with others in order to know them. Anyone who came within fifteen feet of him produced so strong and individualistic (and usually unattractive) a spoor, he could recognize that person in a crowd from then on simply by smell. What's more, he soon learned he could usually tell if they were being truthful, deceitful or secretly hurtful about what they were saying or how they were acting simply from the subtle changes in their odor. While individual, a person's scent varied subtly with emotion. Even more interesting, he could track where they had recently been simply by following their lingering spoor. Over the years, he developed such a memory for smells, he remembered people and events better by recalling their smell than appearance, voice, behavioral quirks or even their taste, though the latter being so closely linked to smell, skin taste was so intense an experience it would be indelibly etched in his mind alongside their smell.

That was especially true of Simi.

But he *wasn't* a bloodhound *or* a dog. Well, not really, in spite of what others still sometimes called him. Looking back, he was, at the tender age of six, simply *uniquely natural*. The problem was that compared to others, he was *exceptionally so*. It all made Rob feel different, isolated, and increasingly reticent to share his experiences with others or join in socially with his less talented group mates.

At twelve, Rob was a strapping five-foot-eight, one-hundred-twenty pounds of lean muscle and sinew. He had shocking green eyes—the eyes he'd been told (he couldn't recall when or by whom) were his father's—a long neck, olive skin, and wavy, shoulder-length, flaming red hair—like his mother (another claim for which he couldn't recall the source). In outdoor sunlight, his olive skin presented as a natural tan that made him the envy of similarly aged girls and boys alike. When he wore his shock of hair in a tight bun he became the ogle of every young female, and to his surprise, of Frann—Billie Frann Frunk to be more exact—the prize jock in his group and increasingly narrow circle of close friends.

An all-round athlete who excelled at any physical sport or game he engaged in, sensitive beyond his years and a rising scholar to boot, Frann was also blatently gay and not afraid of telling everyone so, whether they wanted to hear or not. And Frann acted accordingly. Perhaps it was his open gayness that, like Rob, made him sometimes seem distant, alone and exotic when in fact, quite unlike Rob, Frann could often be found at the center of anything social, surrounded by a gaggle of sighing boys and girls.

From the very first they met at roughly two years of age, Rob and Frann had become close friends and for their subsequent years, studied, talked and hung out together. They had, as everyone jealous of their tight friendship was quick to point out, become *au pair*. Socially, Frann had slowly begun admitting select others into his innermost circle of elitist, mostly gay boys, and, by virtue of being Frann's "best," Rob was tacitly adopted by them. Rob, now painfully shy, was forced to realize he did not and would probably never meet Frann's fundamentally different sexual orientation, leaving Rob at the center of his own inner circle of cute, likable, doting girls. That didn't change his feelings for Frann, however. In essence, Rob slowly became in almost everyone's minds, Frann's "boyfriend" and by implication, though not contract, gay life-partner. In all the girl's eyes he was a sort of James Dean loner, and, it was assumed, heartbreaker. Loner, that is, to everyone except Frann, and a real heartbreaker to Andry.

To be completely honest (something not easily accomplished at his age), to him, Andry had always been more than a friend long before he realized it. Though outwardly a female Frann fan, like Rob, Andry was different than the others. Sort of, anyway. And it was that sense of vague mutual difference that had inexorably drawn the three together from the first time they met.

Raymond Gaynor

Chapter 15

The two Enforcers were locked in anxious discussion. *Odd*, thought Rob. *Why would two Enforcers be anxious? And why here on overnight beat? They must be looking for something...or someone?* He decided to wait longer in hope of uncovering anything additionally unusual before rushing on to work. Shaking his head to clear his mind, he returned back to memories of the early days with his nest mates.

Andry was an unusually precocious, delicate-boned, five-foot-three-inch tomboy: a mess of awkward arms and legs, cute in a fetching impish way. Her boyish athleticism—she could beat anyone who dared to challenge her at virtually all sports—anyone except, she quickly discovered to her unending frustration, Frann. These days, she looked the role, having pixie-cut her long, straight, mousy-brown hair. While most people's eyes were of one predominant color, hers reflected whatever color she or those around her wore. Bright metallic striations overlaid her startling brown pupils that, when struck by sunlight flashed every color of the rainbow, coalescing outside of sunlight when alone and *au naturel* to a deep liquid-brown. Overall this gave her an enigmatic, spiritual ambience that people either immediately liked or disliked. Rob felt drawn to her from their first meeting, but whether she liked anything at all about him back then had been irritatingly unclear. Andry otherwise looked as normal as any other gangly adolescent girl, though her personal custodian, a pear-shaped, dowdy frump who everyone called Wanta, clearly didn't think so. Wanta watched Andry like a hawk, her sharp eyes and tongue were constantly engaged in a seemingly bitter struggle to exercise absolute custodial control over her.

Andry's female mob initially tagged her as a boyish smart-ass, and kept her on the fringe. She didn't seem to notice or care, though Rob could smell concern, a sort of nervousness and alertness that seemed to lurk just beneath the refreshingly cool, outdoorsy smell of her youthful body, and the slowly ripening scent of her coming-of-age. To Rob, she seemed decent: a nice girl with whom he could easily hang out without having to watch his back. Andry in turn was careful to project an air of hesitant self-assurance around Rob. Later, she often reminded him she knew exactly what she liked…and she had always liked him. Well mostly. Sort of.

Rob knew from the sweet harmony of her scent that when she addressed him, she was always telling him the truth. Not many adolescents were like that. Most projected a kind of naive deceitfulness, a subtle off-balancedness, as if they were seeking someone to give them a push-start, or tell them what to think or do.

With each passing day, Rob sensed Andry maturing, until one day she took him entirely by surprise when she started projecting the faintest tinge of his *own* smell. Odd. Startling even. But all in all, a pleasant change. Their growing chemical familiarity was intriguing, increasingly sensual if not quite yet sexually seductive for him.

Rob soon discovered he could not only recognize Andry and Frann's telltale spoors, but he could instantly picture in his mind where they were standing within any group even with the lights out. Moreover, he could tell when either was happy, hungry, sad, angry, frustrated...or interested in someone, including himself.

The pair smelled distinctly different. Being with one, or on more common occasions both was like reading the freshly written pages of an evolving novel. He came to know not only their olfactory signatures and thereby immediate emotions and feelings, but what often they wanted even before they knew themselves, a never ending source of fun and amazement for all three.

On one particularly memorable day, the three were walking vigorously along a favorite road-walkway surrounded by seemingly natural but actually individually named and tended trees, shrubs and flowers. A group of plant sponsors were chatting together in the distance. Andry suddenly leaped from the walkway onto a patch of grass between two particularly large trees. Without thinking, Frann laughingly followed, leaving Rob alone to make a quick decision whether or not to join them. Rob, still walking, abruptly turned and jumped to join them on the same patch of warm, pungent grass.

The three, momentarily out of breath, began laughing and pushing each other, until, during their jockeying, Rob noticed Frann eyeing him and Andry eyeing Frann. He also noticed a particularly heavy mustiness suffusing the air about them, increasing with each of Frann's exhalations, and a similar, though oppositely polar sweet fecundity adding to, mixing in and growing with each of Andry's. It was a golden moment in their lives when each in turn discovered new, awakening feelings for each other.

Frann and Andry continued teasing and pushing each other, but Andry's touches that usually lingered on Frann's flesh, seemed shorter this time, as if she were trying to communicate something important that was eluding her. Frann, in turn, constantly bumped and brushed against Rob while mock-fighting off Andry's increasingly giggly advances, each bump and brush lasting a little longer and always accompanied by a flash of his eyes towards Rob. Rob, losing himself in the heady, fertile aromas of the flowers, trees, grass and their three naked bodies, became entrapped in two richly sensuous, sexually laden daydreams each as real to him as the most professionally designed T-rip.

In one, he lay on the cool green grass curled up next to Frann—suddenly Billie to him—while rays of hot summer sunlight warmed their bodies, odoriferously broadcasting from each intense masculine desire. Everything within Rob wanted to sigh and give himself to Billie. Instead, hovering in desire, he waited expectantly for their dammed up feelings to burst at any moment. Any moment. Each assumed that their two bodies would merge, totally and completely in the strong embrace of the other who truly loved him. The key word was "assumed."

In the other, he towered above Andry—now Simi to him—wanting nothing more than to plunge into her, while she clung fitfully onto him, greedily accepting him.

Startled, Rob—in his mind now Draff to Billie and Simi, who had suddenly stopped their playful bullying and were staring at Draff—looked from one to the other, then dropped his eyes to the trundled leaves of grass, blushingly aware of each's person's body's vaporous acrid pleadings. Draff awkwardly regained his balance and jumped back onto the walkway, head low, Billie and Simi quickly following, the two sliding their arms through Draff's, while calling him softly and lovingly back into the present. Their new, shared present. A new present whose horizons in one brief moment had expanded wider than the omniverse.

Chapter 16

Draff—he was *definitely* Draff to both Simi and Billie after their mutually shared awakening—had not actually engaged in physical sex with either yet, but spent many subsequent hours carefully studying the complex, developing aromas of each of his two assumed-to-be sexual partners, discretely sampling and resampling the air between them, comparing it to that of others in their group until he could close his eyes and instantly identify each's momentary physical desires. Uncanny as it felt, Draff knew at the same time that he was barely scratching the surface of his ability, especially in regard to his two most intimate friends.

By the time they were juniors, each was accustomed to studying alone from his or her teen domicile, uniting holographically by distance, an obvious exception to the general educational system designed to dampen the countless "acting out" problems of adolescence. The mob's educational interests on the other hand had suddenly turned to romance, love, human anatomy, the "how-to" of lovemaking and the many complex ramifications of procreation. All three looked forward to his or her SweetSixteen, when each would be legally empowered to make decisions for themselves without a personal custodian perpetually at the side. It was their moment to stand before society, choose their future identities, leave their adolescent homes, stretch their adult wings and fly.

Draff and Semi's relationship blossomed, becoming close friends, then best friends and helpmates, though at times it seemed to each that they were more like brother and sister than boyfriend and girlfriend. Simi, like Billie, found Draff's ability to anticipate her feelings before she was aware of them increasingly disconcerting, but proved eminently willing to repeatedly forgive him, as his guesses became more and more personal and embarrassingly accurate. Draff could even anticipate her forgiving him: the knowing smile and waving flick of her increasingly slender feminine hand that always followed a momentary waft of invitingly exotic effervescent spice with a balmy, lingering, ambrosial after-smell.

For her part, Simi, during this time, was coming into her own, blossoming like a desert rose after a long awaited, highly anticipated rain. Her short, mousy brown hair deepened into a growing cascade of dark-roasted cappuccino brown, which she began unconsciously tossing. Her face paled and thinned, but at the same time softened.

Her eyes developed an even more, impossible-to-ignore glow that seemed to bathe her face in an I-am-ready-for-motherhood radiance. Her lips became fuller, redder, riper. Her body reshaped, morphing over what seemed mere days into a wanton vessel with two very noticeable breast swells and a suddenly more distinctive feminine curve to her hips. Short, but perfectly proportioned, Simi knew she had finally entered her reproductive years and so did everyone else, Draff included.

At the same time that Draff began noticing her in this new way, Billie became more frustrated with and disinterested in her, instead, publicly reveling in Draff's ability to anticipate his every mood and whim. It was as if he and Draff shared a secret between them that no longer included Simi, the two young men changing from tight comrades and *confidantes* to, as predicted by many who watched them together, either future-fated lovers or competitors, with nothing in between.

Billie, too, was maturing. His lean, almost gawky athletic child-body already attractively muscled, had, from rigorous exercise, developed to Olympic proportions. His dark swarthy face, framed invitingly in tight, wiry, jet-black Grecian curls, accented his increasingly angular cheek bones and solid, perceptively dimpled chin. His chin and cheeks became dusted with the first hint of an afternoon shadow.

His eyes blazed fiercely, like a warrior awaiting the command to ravish the world and savor its spoils.

Billie was in awe of Draff. It wasn't admiration, but a back-of-the-neck hair-prickling kind of awe of Draff's flawless ability to anticipate all his desires. Billie, outwardly gay, had always been and had never hesitated to let people around him know his predilection. Yet there seemed something hidden, buried beneath the outgoing gay veneer. Something carefully and intentionally concealed even from himself, something unconscionable that was increasingly begging for acknowledgement.

Chapter 17

Draff tried desperately to reciprocate Billie's attentions, but inevitably failed. It just wasn't Draff. Painfully aware of each's falterings, Draff and Billie quietly, judiciously parried them into fits of raucously mutual, slide-spitting laughter, followed by quiet appreciation. To each's surprise, repetition, instead of lessening their feelings for each other and separating them, simply deepened their hidden feelings into silent ever-growing affection, but always without overt physical expression. Billie, in frustration, repeatedly "gave up," returning back to simply being himself around other males, in essence signaling Draff what he was pretty certain Draff already knew. Even so, Billie continued to respectfully acknowledge Draff's "special gift," much to Draff's relief and eventual delight, even if that delight were, in the end, destined for another.

Billie soon took to talking openly about wishing they could have more "moments" alone together with a clearly contrived, off-the-cuff jocularity that, of course, fooled no one. Indeed, it wasn't meant to. To others, Billie's open, standing request was more of a sign to himself and others of his increasing maturity and ever solidifying predilection. To Draff, it was a prelude to their increasing number of seemingly serendipitous, but actually mutually planned, quiet, more deeply intimate moments—their own shared, continuously developing, special kind of foreplay.

One such moment eventually ended in light petting, stroking, caressing, and finally, the sharing of a hesitant kiss. Their evolving *repertoire*, coupled with Draff's astute smell awareness, tenaciously escalated the sexual tension that seemed to perpetually surround them like a feral beast with squinting red serpent eyes and an untamable carnal desire quite all of its own.

In Draff's mind, the situation was clearly meant to arouse him into sexual submission, but it had, instead, begun to remind him disquietingly of an incident with a visiting government educator.

On occasion, different educational groups would be holographically, and on special occasions like this one physically brought together for a "special lesson." This time, the instructor, before the enlarged group, began by pointing out Draff Rob Brie as a "sensory freak." After delivering a monolog on "sensory freaks" and the damage they impart to the population "simply by existing," he then stated his intention to prove it not scientifically, but more importantly these days, *socially* by demonstrating to the group how easily such "idiot savants" could be identified. He immediately commanded an assistant he'd brought with him to stand behind Brie and cover his eyes with her hands. He then ordered Brie to sniff each group member as they filed past. Taking up the challenge reluctantly and with trepidation, Brie did as directed, and the instructor then began pointing out the different expressions on Brie's face as a group member passed, implying the differences of expression "proved" not only Brie's profane occult ability, but also his true feelings for each of them (though Brie noted warily that the instructor always describe his supposed "true feelings" in the negative). Jan and Frunk declined to participate, watching with abject horror. It quickly became clear to Brie that the instructor was attempting to isolate him from his group and worse, his mob. While this was happening, the instructor's hesitant female assistant expressionlessly removed her hands from his eyes and took a step back, as if in fear of Brie catching and reacting to *her* smell.

Outwardly captivated but inwardly horrified by the inhumanness of the demonstration and its implications, whenever Brie later resurrected the memory, he caught himself imagining what it would have been like if the aberrantly "normal" instructor had been caught in the act by Enforcers (he hadn't and that still worried Brie), at the same time wondering what it must have been like for the girl who stood behind him, and who, afterwards, was also identified by the "instructor" as an object of equal ridicule for having agreed to participate. In fact, throughout the "demonstration" as the instructor called it to justify his vile actions, Brie was aware from the man's smell that it was the instructor who was the freak. Brie shuddered, wondering what it would have been like to be the instructor, acting out Brie assumed a similar experience of his own, perhaps experiencing scorn, derision or worse, pity, eventually being ostracized. In his vision, he could imagine, with another shudder, it happening to himself. That he could identify with such feelings made him distinctly uncomfortable. The result was that those complex feelings eventually transferred, in spite of his best efforts, into his increasingly physical relationship with another man, namely Billie.

Then there was the instructor's assistant. Afterwards, Brie tried several times to catch her attention, but she quickly averted her eyes, staring blankly elsewhere as if in connecting it might cause her even more embarrassment. Brie could tell from her persistent sour, acrid aroma, that she was much more deeply hurt than she was willing to let appear. In fact, within her mind, having acted on the educator's orders, her seething disgust had fermented into a deep self-loathing. Brie alone realized that while the major focus had been on him, it had also been surreptitiously directed at her. The end result was that both felt publicly humiliated by the instructor in front of the group, and Brie assumed in front of their mobs. Only later was he to learn that her hurt was so much deeper than his, for she *was* an idiot-savant.

Humans are supposed to have four basic tastes: sweet, sour, bitter and salty. Maybe five, if one includes *umami*, identified by the Japanese as something akin to "tongue-touch satisfaction." The girl, however, like the smallest percentage of already rare taste savants, could discern a much wider complement of tastes, and that was only the beginning. The same instructor who had humiliated the two of them, had *previously* disgraced the girl in front of both her group and mob, ordering her to demonstrate how she could identify people, including each of her study mates, by touching her tongue to the subject's skin. Later, Brie would discover that her expanded sense of taste could be initiated by flicking the quivering tip of her tongue in the air like a python near a person or where a person had just been. After the same instructor had debased the two, the girl had smelled to Brie of revulsion—the same revulsion that he smelled issuing from the instructor standing next to him. But it was more than revulsion; It was the fetid odor of a person secretly harboring a death-wish.

There existed individuals with one or more augmented sense, often to the detriment of the remaining senses—true *idiot* savants—the rarest lacking the ability to think rationally or feel emotionally. Later, learning more about the girl's plight, Brie—by choice, Rob to the wounded girl— desperately wanted to placate her hurt, if by nothing else, by pointing out that she was *normal enough* to be included with him in the enviable group of single-sense savants, while her tormentor, he suspected from the intensity of the man's smell, might surreptitiously belong to the latter. Rob wanted to, but she was, he was later to learn, simply too hurt to accept any attempt to reach out to her.

Chapter 18

In truth, Brie could tell from the assistant's scent that she wasn't overly intelligent, at least, not in the way one usually thought of intellect. For instance, when after making an example of Brie, their vicious interlocutor had attempted in front of her group to extract from her a pitifully intimate detailing of her "impairment," she stopped and had to taste his words in the air with a flickering tongue before awkwardly replying. After this "special lesson," her personal custodian—a gruff-spoken, bone-thin, unshaven, wild-eyed man in his late seventies—walked up to her and, staring ashamedly away, further reinforced the instructor's demonstration of her "disgusting ability, if, in fact, she had one at all." The intent, in Brie's eyes, was clearly to vilify her further.

On another occasion when his and her group were holographically blended, members from both groups ignored the instructor and began callously debating in front of the two as to whether the two were, in fact, *very* clever fakes— exceptional Fast Eddies, preying on a crowd's pity for what attention he or she could obtain, or the correctly reviled freaks as the two had been presented. Neither Brie nor the girl would have been the first or the last to try such, one student exclaimed intentionally loud enough for all, including the contrite-appearing girl to hear, and to Brie's dismay, several holographic heads about them nodded in agreement.

After what seemed a long and particularly awkward silence, during which the girl's personal custodian indicated more interest in the ceiling than her well-being—the combined male group members began jeering. When they began pressing in closer about Brie and the girl's projected images, she audibly sighed and to everyone's surprise suggested a "real experiment" to test her skill. The boys, Brie included, hesitated. What she was proposing was a test of her skill *ex-situ*. Holographically. Something to Brie's knowledge had never been done before.

After some discussion, Frunk was directed to locate and return with a stack of tissue squares. Holding them by the edge, Frunk distributed them to each of the holographic boys in the two groups. The girl then instructed each boy to tear off the corner with which Frunk had held the tissue, rub the the tissue between holographic fingers for a moment, and write a secret word on a folded corner before handing them holographically to the girl. While the boys did as instructed, some began daring the girls in the group to do the same.

Frunk left for more tissues.

The girls' take on the "real experiment," however, was entirely different. Not having been directly invited to participate by the solitary female figure before them, they responded grudgingly, acquiescing hesitantly and reservedly one by one, as if concerned that their sister-by-gender might be found to be exactly what the boys obviously suspected—a fake. If she was, the thought of uncovering her in front of a scoffing, sniggering group of boys made some of the girls, especially Jan, who well knew of the complexity of Brie's feelings surrounding his own ability and the uneasiness he generally felt about exposing it directly to others.

It took the girl, pinching her nose with her left hand and flicking her, to everyone's surprise devil-like *bifurcated tongue* above the napkins in her right, one-by-one, less than a second to correctly identify each holographic member's paper. She did it regally, and to everyone including Brie and Jan's awe, perfectly, though Brie noted her hesitate, eyes narrowing briefly when she actually touched Frunk's napkin with a flick of the tip of her slithering pink tongue. Later Billie told Draff he had ignominiously rubbed his piece of the tissue between his thighs.

The result was that the girl earned some respect (alongside a certain mystique) resonating within each learner a different, unique, embarrassingly empathic feeling. Some were absolutely convinced of the genuineness of the girl's unusual, even strange "ability," others of its exceptional nature, while still others held firmly that holographic sensation was simply too outlandish to believe and could only be a *really* clever fake. Simi visibly shuddered. For her, the whole exercise was like bedding another woman and afterwards experiencing a sort of regret for having done so, while at the same time for not having done it sooner, or having actually not done it at all.

Before leaving, the girl called Frunk over and whispered something to him in visibly painful confidence. Frunk never told anyone, even Draff, what the girl said, but everyone who witnessed it agreed that after that Billie Frann Frunk's demeanor toward her permanently changed. Later, Draff would smell an overwhelming respect exuding from Billie that up to then had been exclusively reserved for him. Billie also began regarding and treating Draff differently, with even more awe if that was possible, but, more importantly, with a new, barely perceptible edge of distrust. It was all there in his smell.

Draff found it odd to think of Billie as distrustful, but the unusually extraordinary event had caused Draff Rob Brie [Septican-Smite] to believe even more solidly in his own ability. As for holographic sensation—well, that was something else. The taste savant, for example, had smelled distinctly more post-adolescent than she behaved, dressed or appeared. *So, was it, in fact, all an act? Was her custodian and the derogatory instructor part of the act? Was she actually a really good fake, a SuperFast Eddie like some continued to hold in a league all her own? And if so, why play it out before not just their two particular educational groups but specifically in front of him? And what of Billie?* Draff tried to hold these disquieting thoughts in his head while he re-examined himself and his experiences surrounding *his* unique skill, but the effort proved too complex, and he let it slip and dissipate. She had, he reminded himself, exuded a rich, fecund smell, as if she were over-ripe, likely meaning interested and willing to mate then and there in front of everyone as if the "experiment" had excited her, but with...Billie!? During their previous physical "lesson," Draff's nose had told him that Billie had no sexual interest in her, which, if she could, she surely must have tasted, assuming her extraordinary sense was, as he was inclined to believe, legitimate and even more unusual and developed than his sense of smell. She'd lingered when she brushed the tip of her tongue on Billie's scrap of tissue, and momentarily when she'd holographically tasted the edge of Simi's and his. Had the girl discerned in her tasting of Billie's, Simi's and his slips of paper something about the threesome and their relationship that even he, Draff, hadn't thus far?

The girl, he also noticed, continued eyeing Billie Frann Frunk [Tordon-Cass] closely out of a corner of one eye while the holographic lesson closed and everyone prepared to disapparate. Then she watched Brie's image with what seemed to him an increasingly uncomfortable interest… licking the air, and, he noticed anxiously, sniffing it as well. Was she trying to indicate to him she alone was aware of the true extent of *his* unique gifts? Or was she, in fact, secretly able to both taste *and* smell?

The bouquet she broadcast when they first met had had surprisingly no place in it for him. Their smells seemed to him like dissonant symphonies, by their very nature incapable of harmonizing, destined to waft on in hopes of resonating with others more compatible. Everything about her was yet another in what was to prove a long line of surprises, and he felt for a fleeting instant like the freak he imagined she felt, her aroma suggesting that she regarded him him similarly.

Chapter 19

Later that evening, Draff and Billie were walking together through one of thousands of brightly lit, thickly crowded commercial walkways, pausing every so often to respond to one or another personalized verbal advertisement message—P-VAM for short—activated by their individual biometrics as they passed by the myriad hidden sensors. Listening absentmindedly to the personalized enticements to buy, buy, buy the very things that at that moment they could from all the data gathered and statistically calculated want (and just barely afford), each advertisement sounded like it was being whispered to him for him alone by a trusted *confidente*.

It was good to stroll leisurely together, off-handedly, impulsively, like this, while items of possible interest, based on their needs, wants and desires—and equally on their lifelong recorded purchase history—were softly being brought to their attention. They could, of course, respond if they wished, simply by a look, a word, or finger flick, thereby placing an order, and the ordered item would most likely be waiting, gorgeously wrapped—based again on their individual preferences—at their domicile courtesy of QTrans when each arrived home.

Billie, excited to hear about a new shade of body makeup, slipped his palm into Draff's. Draff accepted it nonchalantly but willingly. It seemed hard for Draff to imagine the days when people who wanted to share a moment of physical contact had been scared to hold hands in public. It was so...relaxing. Draff sighed, smiled and rested his head against Billie's rippling bicep.

Billie stopped in front of one of their favorite Azuki shops, and awkwardly attempted to explain as offhandedly as he could, how much he "really liked" Draff...better even than that girl with the amazing ability to taste things. It seemed a dry, somewhat incongruous compliment, coming out more like sarcasm than affection to Draff, and Billie's smell confirmed it was sarcasm, at least in part. Yet...there was something decidedly more to Billie's comment than mixed compliment and sarcasm. Beneath the macho boy-to-boy patina that Billie strove so hard to maintain, Draff detected something subtly, longingly, mesmerizingly desirous: a steaming warmth that Draff realized he had been waiting for a long time to sense from Billie.

Billie stretched an arm around Draff's shoulders and whispered in his ear that he'd never found another as attractive as he found Draff.

Draff felt momentarily confused. Had Billie been so unaware of their growing relationship as to be all the time half-actively looking elsewhere? *An odd question for me to ask myself,* Draff thought, *given our different sexual predilections.*

Draff's confusion dissolved, however, the moment he noticed an increasing randiness in Billie's odor. Despite his own limited experience, it was clear that Billie desired him. Here. Now. Draff thought to himself with a smile that each was "sniffing the other out," like one dog might sniff another to see if the other was receptive. *If Billie can't smell my desire, then,* Draff thought, *what does that make Billie? An intelligent brute? Did he honestly not smell even a whiff of Draff's admittedly reticent desire, and, if not, how then could Billie ever know with any certainty—and, oh yes, he clearly did—if any other was sexually interested in him?*

Draff laughed nervously. He'd met enough intelligent brutes to know that relationships between him and them would never work. Draff had, over the years learned a particularly painful lesson: to avoid more than friendly liaisons with non-special people. To avoid their intricate entrapments, their odd sense of normalcy, just as he learned to not allow himself to get too close to extraordinarily unusual people like the "idiot savant" girl. That doesn't leave much, Draff thought, so is that why am I letting, no, encouraging Billie like I am?

In fact, Billie's touch just felt good. Just plain good. Really. Perhaps, Draff wondered, after a particularly pleasing caress by Billie's strong hand down the side of his tensing abdomen, he was being too self-judgmental. Perhaps in the end, he, Draff, was after all *partially* gay? Was there such a thing? Or maybe bisexual? That was a possibility. Or maybe it had something to do with his gift? Or maybe his gift had something to do with his feeling particularly receptive to this man whose warm breath on his ear was making his face redden? Why not? It made as much sense as anything else in this world.

In spite of his musings, Draff's body acquiesced to the strong arm about him, and Billie responded by pulling Draff closer and firmer against him. Draff, ear pressed against Billie's barrel chest, could hear and feel the faster than usual beat of his friend's heart. Thump-thump, thump-thump, thump-thump—the sound unexpectedly reminded him of his mother's heartbeat when he was still in the womb.

As Billie's grip tightened, Draff felt his tension release. His mind, floating in a narcotic cloud, drifted back to that past, misty, empyrean time before the *event*. Before all the madness started. *Odd*, Draff thought in passing. *Odd how vivid these earliest experiences from the womb. Maybe chalk it up to the other anomaly?* His enhanced memory seemed as bizarre as his special smell ability, and now the—what else could he call it—man-attraction thing. *What kind of a freak am I?* he thought, a ripple of panic momentarily tearing though the velvet memories he had become momentarily lost in, wondering if they or he had stepped over a line from which there would be no return. Pleasure. Safety. All his bodily needs, wants and desires attended. What was this feeling? Love? Draff felt himself blush warmer and leaned deeper into Billie's arms. Billie liked—no, passionately desired—him and maybe even could end up loving him as a soul mate. *Were they similar enough to be soul mates?* Draff wondered, noting Billie's increasingly potent and focused desire. But love? Not just physical need or longing, but spiritual love? Ah, well, that was *much* more complex, subtle and elusive than a body's momentary desire. And without a sense of smell like his, how could anyone know anything for certain? Even with his gift, Draff couldn't be *absolutely* sure. Letting go yet again of the many opposing deliberations in his mind, he snuggled his nose into the hollow of Billie's throat and breathed deeply, hoping that somehow, someway, someday the feelings of uncertainty would flee and he would know for certain.

Raymond Gaynor

Chapter 20

Feeling Draff close, a thrill of pure adrenaline coursed through Billie. It had never been a problem being forthright with others about being gay, but embracing Draff's warm, delectable, nubile body, all the words, all the things he had so wanted to say to Draff, not as a friend but as a lover, instantly flooded, then escaped him. *That is perhaps the real difference between us,* Billie thought silently to himself. *I know myself. I've been flaming hot for him all along, while he's been literally years in simply awakening to his deepening innate desire for me. I don't need a whatcha-ma-call-it-super-sense to know he wants me. And now, pressed against me like this, relishing at last his own long-smoldering desire, I...I don't know what to do. I don't want to hurt my tenderhearted best-friend, so vulnerable, melting like warm butter in my arms, ready perhaps at last for the taking.* There was the rub: "perhaps." That instant discord between desire, will and action.

Draff swung his arms up, entwined his fingers behind Billie's neck, and looked dreamily up into Billie's sparkling eyes, toying with the mass of soft curls on the back of Billie's head. *He wants me.* Draff knew this without doubt. Billie's spicy pungentness had become heavier, like the weight of Billie's body Draff could imagine pressing on top of him, surrounding him, probing for an entrance into his innermost being. Breaths shortening, pulses quickening, Draff felt the first hint of dewy moisture form on the back of Billie's pulsing neck, and, in a moment of total abandon, Draff threw back his head, closed his eyes and let go, allowing once again, everything within him to change as it would.

This kind of inner metamorphosis had become the norm during the decades since the birth of NewAmerica. Two-parent families, now *passe*, had outlived their usefulness long before the great reorganization that Jackson and Draff's personal hero, Adelphous "Addie" Tripler, had ushered in. Nowadays, marriages were typically two-year contracts during which the procreators—heteros or "alternative" same-sex—agreed to pool resources and work together to assist their offspring—natural, adopted or assigned—until the children were old enough to be enjoined to a social family. Social families, or "nests" as they were popularly called, quickly become a universally accepted con.

Au pairs could contract directly with the state to care for up to five children born of other parents. In return, the state would comp them expenses and a generous sally. It was a highly sought after billet and a pair's pros were examined and re-examined carefully by the state before authorizing such.

Under a standard two-year contract, partners were permitted to con with up to three additional nests, in some instances, like Rob's, sharing the same physical domicile, creating natural groups. To ease tensions, contracted pairs not uncommonly took on outside lovers of the same, opposite, null or indeterminate sex. ContraSpray, after all, worked in any of the above situations.

In practical terms, New Americans, at the urging of the state, rediscovered and eventually came to fully embrace the concept of the extended family, and it proved the salvation of social NewAmerica. After two years, bios, it was said, began investing too much of their thoughts and behaviors in their children, becoming simply too close and the state too distant from the chldren, nests providing the perfect social atmosphere for children to grow, develop and thrive both individually and collectively after the minimum two years. In time, each individual's expanded social network would prove immensely valuable to cope with the myriad of choices that NewAmerica, NewTerra, the national planets and the artificial orbital stations surrounding them, as well as the universe itself would present.

Most bios, like Draff's, let their children go at exactly two years of age, thought by most socio-psychologists to be the optimal developmental age for the child to most quickly adjust and assimilate into a social nest. Draff's first social nest was a closely-knit, a full-fledged "three" duly registered with the state under the trademark, "First One," a semi-acronym for First Organizational Network Enterprise based on the strong leadership role these particular caretaker "parents" were contracted to develop in Rob, Andry and Frann while they was under their care.

Draff never knew the names of his bios, and, in all honesty, it hadn't ever seemed that important, given the challenges of adjusting to and growing up in his new social nest. All he really knew was that his first *social* or custodial father—"sho-ef," one of millions of "Smites"—was a co-caretaker of three other social nests, and his sho-em— one of tens of thousands of "Septicans"—was part of two. For egalitarian reasons, custodians were not permitted to know the names of any of their ward's bios. All together over the past years, his sho-ef had taken sixteen lovers and his sho-em five. The result was that Draff Rob Brie [Septican-Smite] grew up with biological brothers and sisters (if any) entirely unknown to him, and a complement of forty-eight primary social brothers and sisters. If one counted the various relations through all his social parents' opposite and same-sex lovers as well, Rob had an additional eighty-plus social cousins with whom he had most likely met or at least come into holographic contact at one time or another. As bios and custodians typically also served as sho-ef's and sho-em's for other's children at one time or another, the size of Brie's social network could easily count in the thousands if not more. That's what "social" meant in the new world.

Draff's current nest-mob was trademarked "Trio Safe Prime"—nicknamed rather than acronymed "The Trinity"—and consisted of Brie, Frunk and Jan. While their choice to live and grow together had seemed serendipitous, there had always been, looking back, something providential, fated—destined—in their meeting and bonding, and they each felt it deeply.

Draff recalled the day he met Billie, or more correctly, the day Billie met him. Draff/Rob/Brie was playing alone in a large sandbox. After awkward mutual introductions, they had begun playing side-by-side, acting as best they could at so young and tender an age as if totally disinterested in each other. Billie/Frann/Frunk, from out of nowhere, had reached over and grabbed—borrowed as Billie always recounted it later—a block from out of Draff's hands. It was a tense meeting, each stunned at discovering his interest in the other, each wondering what the other would do. The moment the shock wore off, they resumed their playing but together instead of separately, beginning an instant friendship that would last the rest of their lives.

Actually, Billie proved the perfect counterfoil to Draff's reserve. Billie was blatantly outgoing in every sense of the word: physically, emotionally, psychologically…and sexually. It was really no surprise to either that they had begun exploring sex with each other, mostly at Billie's prompting and with Draff's initially hesitant but eventually willing acquiescence, Draff's loneliness and curiosity eventually getting the better of the many amorphous fears that seemed to always be hovering around him.

Draff liked Billie the moment he first smelled him. Billie's fragrant, tangy aura enjoined them like two, piquant complementary spices—Draff's cinnamon to Billie's nutmeg—their increasing physical intimacy being the perfect topping. It was during a moment of mutual naked physical exploration that Simi, who had been hovering about Billie ever since the two boys had met, inserted herself between them. It was another tense meeting, Draff, Billie and Simi each being stunned at discovering the other's physical differences, each staring at the other wondering what the other could and would do, each for different reasons.

For Draff, it was Simi's spring-like bouquet—a dash of ginger—added to the spicy combination that made the three, together, seem complete. For Billie, it was a combination of Simi's boyish directness and the flash of her wide-eyes that reflected in them what he as yet barely knew he wanted from Draff. For Simi, it was Billie's audacious aplomb and Draff's silent, brooding, magnetic, almost mystical insightfulness. Mysterious Simi, rebellious Billie, sensitive Draff became an instant trefoil, inseparable from that moment on.

Raymond Gaynor

Chapter 21

Draff and Billie, as they quickly approached SweetSixteen, had abruptly taken to clothing themselves. Draff this evening—the night of their SweetSixteen—had chosen a breezy, chiffon-like, throwaway paper top. No shimmering colors that sensed one's skin temperature or changed color to reflect one's mood. Just a soft, cream-colored, translucent, poncho-like top draped over a perfect replica of a pair of classic skin-hugging, "blue jeans," his concession to modernity being that there was only one pant leg and he went barefoot. Going barefoot was something Draff recently discovered to be sensually intriguing. His current nest mob, namely Billie and Simi, on the other hand, thought it boring enough to stare briefly at his bare left leg and both feet, and then disregard them entirely, a response which, given Draff's current notoriety, he happily approved.

Billie had chosen a brilliant, iridescent-green, skin-tight, opaque, one-piece jump suit that made him, in Draff's opinion, look like a giant lizard on the prowl, which was in fact, exactly how Billie felt that evening and wanted to appear. Neither bothered with "underwear," it having been gladly given up long prior to these times. In deference to Draff's repeated suggestion—*nagging* Billie had loudly and unceremoniously called it—Billie also walked barefoot. It made them, in Draff's mind at least, a complementary two-some.

Draff slipped a toe inside the ankle end of Billie's jumpsuit, and Billie grinned ear-to-ear. The impression to passersby would be one of innocent, serendipitous teasing, though it wasn't at all as innocent or serendipitous as it appeared. Both had practiced petting together all week, just for their joint SweetSixteen. In spite of all the preparation that had gone into this "first" and admittedly determinative "date," each honestly felt that he was spontaneously enacting what fate had brought them together to inevitably do.

After graduating into their second social nest, every child at four years of age was assigned in addition to his or her contracted social custodians, a personal *state* custodian, a PerCust. The PerCust's responsibility was to ensure the bios' recorded wishes for their children were met, serving not in their stead, but as a "watchdog"—a legal state guardian, protector, advisor, and, if the match was a particularly good one, mentor and friend, until the child at SweetSixteen became a self-sufficient adult. This was, of course, in addition to the various contracted social custodians and holographic educators selected by the state *with the requisite approval of the PerCust*, a delicate everyday balance of power meant to assist the child in developing to its fullest potential while serving as a model for the future child's adult behavior.

The norm was one PerCust per child for the full twelve years, as was the case with Billie and Simi. Draff, on the other hand, ended up having *five* consecutive PerCusts, all of whom at one time or another had to be replaced.

Whoever in the world has five PerCusts? Draff mused depreciatively to himself, half-frowning, half-smiling, while checking the night ground weather, more a nervous gesture than anything else, given the ground weather in the urban corridors at night never varied: dark, cloudy and pleasantly cool till three in the morning, then chilly, light rain till five and a return after that to bright, partly cloudy and warm day. Most kids, like the idiot-savant girl who he could never forget, enjoyed—in her case perhaps suffered less—for having only one PerCust, irrespective of the contracted social custodian's apparent demeanor. The whole PerCust system was admittedly idyllic, and even in this enlightened social age, it sometimes didn't work.

In the idiot-savant girl's case, for example, Draff wondered why, although her contracted social custodian's perfidity had resulted in her being put on ignominious display and publicly mocked at what Draff assumed had been multiple times, her PerCust had allowed it. Had the event *actually* been staged by the state for her or his mob or educational groups' edification as the visiting instructor had suggested, or was there something darker and more insidious behind the incident?

Either way, Draff took it as a personal warning as to what might happen to *him* should his gift—or curse depending on how one looked at it—become a state labeled social anathema, or worse, a public outrage. On the other hand, perhaps it had nothing at all to do with him, and the incident was simply a cruel punishment for something *she* had done, or the attention was contrived to serve her, her custodian or her PerCust and maybe even the instructor's opaque sally interests. Then again, perhaps it was meant to be an unforgettable generic warning about what happens if one became too obviously "different" in contemporary society. *Not everything in NewAmerica was as evolved as the state liked to make it sound,* thought Draff silently to himself. *No, not at all.*

Rob's first PerCust had been a kind, gentle man, a real surrogate father…until the man was confronted with Rob's "gift." Draff could still recall the day when the man had caught Rob sniffing him, and realized that his charge was an "oddity" unwilling or unable to control his aberrant behavior in public with deportment or, at worst, a recidivist out-of-control uni-sensory idiot-savant freak like the girl who would later haunt Draff. Without further word, the man simply turned and walked out of the nest to never return. It had hurt Rob deeply, but, he consoled himself over the years with the thought that perhaps it was for the better, given that Rob had garnered from the hapless man's scent that there was something "odd" about the PerCust as well. The PerCust was found dead several days later. The newsflash reported that the man had died with a look of horrified surprise fixed on his wide-eyed face.

Rob took the incident personally, assuming the man's terror-in-death to be a reflection of a deep loathing for Rob-the-Freak. In a simple childish way appropriate to his age, Rob concluded that *he* had killed the PerCust. He hadn't meant to, of course, and he didn't really know *how* he had done it. He must, he surmised, be lethal to anyone he allowed to get too close.

Draff and Billie walked hand-in-hand down the dark public corridor to the busiest community street, and stopping, faced each other, allowing their feelings to warm, ignoring Simi and their group mates who, accompanying them, had stopped to watch. The two boys carefully maintained their distance, whispering to each other in hushed tones in anticipation of what they assumed they and everyone there were about to experience: two young bucks swept together in a tide of mutual lust, about to impulsively engage in what promised to be nothing less than the public fornication event of the year. Draff could already hear their names being whispered in the rapidly growing crowd about them in nothing less than total awe.

In the not so distant past, voyeurism had been, by definition, a strictly covert, universally frowned upon endeavor. In NewAmerica, voyeurism occurred overtly in public, and quickly become one of the hottest forms of modern "reality" entertainment. More engaging even than three-dimensional-projected-holovision, one didn't have to be a sensory savant to be swept into the grunts and groans, the arch and plunge of sweet, young, virile bodies engaged in that most human of activities, promising to breathlessly elevate the lucky viewers into their own personal world of mental ecstasy, in the process hopefully reanimating their own sex lives. For the enactors, it held the prospect of the tantalizingly exhibitionistic thrill of public SalsaSex, as SweetSixteeners often called the act itself. In Draff and Billie's case, it held the additional allure of "alternative" sex, an experience both Draff and Billie were at this moment preparing to share with any and everyone willing to take a moment, and, by enjoying the show, participate indirectly in their ecstatic, coming-of-age moment.

Raymond Gaynor

Chapter 22

For modern lovers, SweetSixteenSalsaSex, when it really clicked, especially when virginal and alternative as in the case of Draff and Billie, offered the enactors a further reward: that all-time most sought-after prize of publiczed intimacy, the exceptional, elusive, once-in-a-lifetime "FirstLoveIConsumated" pop emotag, FLIC. While the best in human literature for the last 2,000 years was replete with tales of persistent love, affection and romance—with only occasional consummation, and even rarer ribald sex—it was only during the last decade that transitioning NewAmerica, unquestionably in the throes of the greatest socio-technological changes of any time in history (the government and youth had already taken to referring to them as "advents" for significant cultural advances)—that sex became acknowledged for its own, as both the reason for and outcome of affection and romance. In the process, the public came to know and passionately embrace FLICs as a new interplanetary obsession. The pre-Jacksonian equivalent of a FLIC—unrequited first love—had, for centuries, besotted the written annals of common, everyday romance books with a typically unsavory outcome. Only recently had NewAmericans elevated such stories above romance to an entirely new plane, and, more recently, a new art form. In spite of what people might say in front of one another or in a familiar crowd, it was the opportunity to see and experience a FLIC first hand that drew everyone irresistibly to the various seemingly spontaneous SweetSixteenSalsaSex exhibitions that popped up in the streets, and, as in the case of Draff and Billie, attended by the participants' entire social group. FLIC's, however, were equally common on a popular rock in a park—there were special ones dedicated to SalsaSex in the park nearest Draff's current home—or on an outdoor cafe table, or at work on the boss' desk, always quickly attended by any interested passersby.

Draff and Billie's was to be in the night under a huge strawberry moon, the two projecting their FLIC to the entirety of humanity in lurid, natural-realtime-local and distant-asynchronous-holographic detail. It was through FLICs in all their diverse forms that normal, common, average, everyday NewAmericans on and off planet, satisfied their addiction to the thrill of stumbling on a couple in *delecto flagrante,* much like the ancient Romans satisfied their blood-lust at colosseum events. And being a well-known entertainer, whatever Brie was engaged in, people watched, listened to, scanned for, and in Draff's special case, sniffed out, his SweetSixteen would, it was universally assumed, be the greatest.

So, on a street of their choice, in the long shadows of the night, with a full moon peering on, Draff placed the palms of his hands together as if in prayer, and slowly knelt in front of Billie to the rapidly growing crowd of onlookers' oohs and ahhs, clearly worshiping the man who, it was clear to all, would be his virginity's undoing. Draff's hands raised, then parted; lowering to rest on either side of Billie's hips, elevating public anticipation of how, exactly, the man who everyone assumed would be his undoing, would shortly impale him.

Billie was supposed to invitingly rotate his hips to further the audience's escalating excitement as the moment went "live" throughout the universe, but, in fact, he was, in his mind, no longer acting. The air was heavy with the smell his eager randiness, and it proved a thick, heady perfume, begging Draff to stop waiting for him, and to grasp and pull Billie closer to the initial position that together they had planned so carefully.

Billie groaned loudly and millions of holographic viewers surrounding them groaned with him. As if on cue, Billie, his lizard skin covered haunches sparkling in the kaleidescope-like strobe of recording lights flashing about them, finally thrust his pelvis forward. An awed silence descended, like a thick woolen blanket, and wrapped around the two boys being viewed thoughout the universe. Not one person in their immediate group, despite jostling for a better view, dared breathe.

Realizing Billie was paralyzed by the blaze of recording light all about them, Draff placed his hands behind Billie's waist, pulled him closer, and the first enthralling step in the carefully planned out but not yet enacted primeval dance of the widely broadcast Draff-Billie FLIC began.

The crowd pressed in, hungering for more. The scents and the "ahh's" from the exponentially increasing physical audience seemed to Draff like a collective in-breath, pushing away his anxiety, ripping away his self-consciousness, leaving his base animalistic desire ready to act. Billie, also clearly in another world, once again began gently rocking his hips. The rest is, as they say, history.

Was it, Draff wondered, the true beginning of a shared FirstLove as the eventual millions of faceless people and projections about them were busily fantasizing? Was it the next stride towards a deeper, more physically committed relationship? Was it a first gesture towards becoming soul mates? Or would the man standing before him prove to be just another in a long line of future lovers he would end up part-enjoying, part-suffering in his journey to find true love and his life mate? Brie fell silent, curious about what his first PerCust would have said, and what his and Billie's nest mate, Simi, might be thinking just now.

The day after SweetSixteen proved to be hell. Draff, after the initial flush of notoriety created by his and Billie's *almost*-FLIC—more of that in a moment—had passed, Draff completely withdrew, and everyone in his group became concerned. The collective concern was just short of erupting into some unspecified spontaneous group action—any action, as long as it shook their leader out of his ennui, or as the more sartorial members joked "out of his Frunk"—when a pretty, young, medic assigned by the state to be his fifth and final PerCust appeared. His group mates, noting her attractiveness, took "action," discussing her supposed role openly in front of him much like the two groups had in front of him and the idiot savant girl. Why would the government, they asked, provide a *medical specialist*, especially an attractive *female* medical specialist at this particular time? Was the state trying to say something in regard to him, Billie, his mob and group? It was never a good idea to waken the usually soporific state, so the answer quite simply eluded everyone including Draff, though whatever the intent, he felt certain it had something to do with his first PerCust's sudden death and whatever it was that the state had, he suspected, been trying to tell him—them—with his three successive PerCust's and the idiot-girl-savant demonstration. It couldn't be related to his and Billie's FLIC, or if you preferred, non-FLIC. Or could it?

Rob's fifth PerCust exuded a strong, chlorine odor like pine-scented disinfectant, entirely masking her "natural" smell. Effectively denied use of his special sense, Rob grew increasingly curious, slowly crawling out of his shell, in the end liking her, as her presence challenged him to develop and utilize his other senses. Suddenly having to rely on his other senses slowly drew him back. And what he could discern from the very rare and brief occasions when he caught just a whiff of her *au naturel* told him that she liked him, too.

A week after the now infamous FLIC, while walking behind him on an outing, she touched her finger to a "cultivated natural" rose, nicking her skin and began to bleed. Uncontrollably. In spite of everything Rob and the first responsers—FResps—did, the bleeding wouldn't stop. She died a short time later in agony, diagnosed with a form of allergic sensitivity to that particular species of rose that, according to the government hospital's official public report, had "neutralized her coagulation system" (which triggered an investigation into the particular cultivated natural rose on which she had pricked her finger. The result:

The rose was incinerated, its genetic line obliterated, the roses genetic code removed from the I-Cares vault, and the plant's registered caretaker, to the caretaker's relief, was absolved of all further responsibility.

The incident wracked Rob's soul. He hadn't even once been able to fully catch the PerCust's scent—in Rob's world, to "know" her—before she was gone. What he had smelled of her hadn't hinted of genetic abberation. It didn't make sense, and, as such, it fed his secret nightmare. Here was additional evidence that he was anathema to anyone he allowed close to him, and he began agonizing over his lifelong friend and SweetsixteenSalsaSex partner's future well-being.

Thinking back, his second and third PerCusts hadn't lasted much longer or fared better than this one, at some point abruptly changing in smell and behavior before dying or, at the least, ignominiously exiting. His second PerCust had been a well-known professional who prided himself on taking on difficult cases—a practical sort of fellow who had a gift for attuning to those around him. "Attuning" meaning in *every* way. This was a man it was rumored w h o could truly "walk in another's shoes." After the first PerCust debacle, the nest had been atwitter with rumor and innuendo. Rob's nest mates expressed surprise when word spread that the new PerCust had been assigned to "work specifically" with Rob. That is, Rob was to be his one and only assignment. Despite, or perhaps because of the PersCust's caution, everything went initially well. Until, out of the blue, the man's appearance and behavior altered. Screaming suddenly at Rob about "shades of dark and light time," two Enforcers alerted by Rob's worried nest mates ended up having to forcibly haul the raving man away. As they dragged him out the door, the man fixed a wild-eyed stare on Rob, pointed a shaking finger at him and muttered unintelligibly. The moment the stare broke, the man's body began shaking, his mouth frothing, until the room about Rob smelled of mixed dread, terror and vomit. The man screamed obscenities at the top of his lungs as he disappeared out the door, and Rob never heard from of of him again. All his PerCust's terms of service, some shorter, other's longer, ended differently, but they all shared one thing: Their time with him always ended darkly and abruptly.

Hovering anxiously at the sidelines as the FResps carried the limp, bloodied body of his fifth PerCust away, Draff sought hopelessly for Billie. Though Billie quickly appeared holographically next to him, their eyes never met, their hands couldn't touch, they never exchanged words. Instead the vision of Billie *sans* smell, with a look of split love, concern and fear, furtively dematerialized. Draff swallowed hard, wiped the tears from his eyes, and vowed to crawl back in his shell and this time, never come out.

Raymond Gaynor

Chapter 23

Billie braced himself with a hand against the towering plate of storefront glass. Shivering in the night air, he imagined for a moment the sight he must be presenting to the shoppers *inside* the whole-block-occupying, megalithic, 200-story "low-rise" 24-hour BOPIS ("Buy anything" in this case sexual "online and pickup in store") warehouse front. Laughing nervously, he sighed, shook his head in disbelief, and turned his thoughts back to his lover, Draff, kneeling before him.

SweetSixteenSalsaSex was proving much harder than he had imagined, and apparently infinitely harder for him than for Draff to proceed with making FirstLove in public. Billie willed the uneasiness curdling his stomach to leave through his shakey legs and out into the unwavering concrete beneath his bare feet. Taking a deep breath, he cleared his mind and refocused his thoughts yet again on the seemingly fearless, willing lover before him begging to be taken.

The crowd's amassed carnal desire, pressing ever closer

and harder, willed him to seize the opportunity and finish the job. Billie, again hesitating, noticed an Enforcer stop near the distant the edge of the crowd. The Enforcer, face hidden behind an opaque black face mask, its body hidden beneath a swirl of black, was slowly pushing his way forward through the crowd, presumably to investigate.

Billie gulped and hesitated yet again though this time for a totally different reason than before. He didn't like Enforcers. The crowd, as yet unaware of the Enforcer, took the flick of fear in Billie's eyes for passionate ardor, and a woman at the front, flushed with sexual anticipation, pulled out a bottle of ContraSpray. A vague hiss, and a vaporous cloud appeared in front of her. Thrusting her face into its center, she breathed deeply. A man and a woman to either side of her poked their faces into the disappearing mist and copied her in an attempt to take in the added ambrosia their neighbor was so kindly providing.

Two other onlookers, in front and to Billie's left slipped on CandyShades, their sudden grunts and pelvic thrusts betraying the perceptual shift the glasses were adding to what was yet to unfold before them. Others, in the now massive yet ever growing crowd eagerly joined, lost in their own T-rips.

Billie, feeling Draff's hands on his butt cheeks, reached forward and grasped Draff, stood the two of them upright and turned Draff around to face the awestruck crowd. It was time. Any further delay and, by Billie's calculation, Draff and he might begin to lose both initiative and crowd.

Two youths, both young girls, who Billie guessed from their arrogant hand-on-hip stances were most likely planning a SweetSixteenSalsaSexcapade of their own, pointed at the two young men and giggled. *Jackson!* thought Billie, his focus once again dissolving. The girls, seeing his dismay, continued pointing and giggled louder.

An elderly, hunchbacked woman, standing beside the two girls, irritated by the distraction, extended her arm and vigorously shoved the girls' pointing fingers aside to grunts of approval from adjacent members of the crowd. The girls, reproved, should have silenced and repented, but from where he stood, Billie could see they were exchanging completely unrepentant smirks. The one, head lowered, glanced furtively forward and sideways, winked at Billie and grinned while sliding a hand inconspicuously onto her companion's gyrating thigh. With the other hand, she reached in a pocket and pulled out her own palm-size vial of ContraSpray, releasing its contents and smiling wickedly.

Like a stalking tiger, the translucent cloud, reflecting recording lights and the brilliant full moon above, shimmered like a ghost as the cloud drifted from the girls towards Billie. Transfixed, Billie and the crowd watched its collective, misty rainbow-refractions reach and engulf him and Draff.

Draff, waiting impatiently for Billie's next move, felt the chemically familiar fog enter his lungs and began wrestling to keep his consciousness, while a distant, gnawing growl in the back of his head he hadn't known was even there fought its way forward. Though vague, there was something important about the semi-formed thought, which, in the end coalesced into a memory, that, if only he could shake loose of the effects of the girl's ContraSpray for a moment, he might allow himself to recall, return to, and, in the process, uncover what made it so important. Draff braced his body in the present, closed his mind as best he could to the ContraSpray, shut eyes to the increasingly infatuated crowd and forced himself to let his mind wander where it needed to to identify the memory while waiting...

Rob's third PerCust had been a "spiritual healer," but to Rob and his mob's consternation turned out to be more of an exorcist. Rob sighed audibly, thinking back on his fourth PerCust's term. From a more adult perspective, it was inevitable, but back then it had seemed to him a desperate act by the state to fit an untoward child into the prevailing social system, this time cleverly, adroitly implying, "if-this-one-doesn't-work-out-you're-done-for.".

Actually this one—a stunning native American in her mid-30's—turned out to be gentle, kind, caring, knowledgeable, wise and, to his combined surprise and relief, quite interested in him. She was constantly questioning, challenging and testing him intellectually, emotionally, socially as well as both religiously and spiritually. Every week or so, she'd spend a day meditating, then write up her findings and send them off to her unidentified superiors by QTrans. Most importantly, she openly acknowledged his unique talent and was willing to openly explore with him all its varied implications.

Rob, in turn, developed a crush on her, his first, best, and only, in his mind, *real* PerCust. Though nothing sexual ever came of it (she was, if anything, always overly respectful in Rob's mind), but some of his best memories would be of his romantic infatuation during this singularly happy time of his otherwise troubled childhood.

It wasn't until he confided his love to her that things began to go awry. She began having trouble focusing and the "dark moments" he had experienced with other custodians began appearing. The "problem" in this case was that as she and he explored Rob's sense of smell and its implications, his affinity for her increased, even soared, until one day he caught her staring blankly at him, a dull, wide-eyed, idiot-like look on her face. It only lasted a moment—the merest flicker of a second—then she shook her head, tousled her long, straight, black hair, and continued as if nothing had happened.

The longer they worked together, however, the stronger his feelings for her became, and the more frequent and prolonged the staring episodes become, increasingly taking on an other-world character as if she were being taken over by someone or something decidedly malevolent. Brie sensed it from the profound though momentary changes in her smell that inevitably accompanied the trances. At the very times when Rob's sense of smell seemed to him at its keenest, she had to wrestle hardest to shake out of it. She lasted the longest of all his PerCusts, one day to be taken away in a particularly severe trance from which she couldn't seem to rouse by a pair of emotionless Enforcers.

Change is the nature of life, she taught Rob to repeat like a mantra to himself when things seemed most challenging for him and later, when her trances became more serious and he felt anxious. He recited it without ending as the two deadpan Enforcers carried out his favorite PerCust in front of his assembled and increasingly wary group members. After that, Rob's mantra transformed into brooding self-examination. *Don't all people change over time?* he asked himself, tears stinging his eyes. Because of her, he was being forced to recognize a frightening truth: It was not she who was changing. Put simply, his effect, whatever it was on those he allowed close to him was steadily increasing while his sense of smell sharpened.

While even as a young child, Rob could sense changes in himself, he was left once again with no idea how, why or into what he was changing. All he knew for certain at that time was that he was changing in a way that was common to, and yet entirely different from similar-aged mates, male and female. He could smell a stew of potent new smells boiling within each of them, himself included, and wondered if the changes were a natural part of growing up, and if any were connected to the incidents with custodians. The trouble was, he no longer had anyone "safe" to inquire of—to talk to—no one in whom he could confide his dark fears. Not even his best friends, Frann and Andry, for if he did, he feared he might lose them, too.

Rob's "problem" seemed to crop up whenever someone was empathically close, and the effect showed no signs of relenting as he entered the dazzlingly confusing period of pubertal change. He was physically growing, and parts of him were changing like an emboldening caricature. His jaw was squaring. His voice was deepening. He was developing the first hints of a morning shadow. It was as if a poltergeist had appeared from some dark corner of his mind and was struggling to possess him, to take over his body, his thoughts, his needs, his wants and desires. All this, while his special power of smell continued increasing.

For the moment, whatever it was that was causing his PerCusts (but, interesting point: not his regular custodians) problems, it was biding time, flexing its muscles and testing its sinews, waiting for the right moment—whenever that right moment might be—to ennervate every cell of his body and transform him, ripping away his childhood and adolescence, substituting in their place the awesomely complex state of manhood. *But what kind of man*, Draff's brain suddenly realized he was mouthing, *am I becoming? What kind of new freak am I metamorphosing into?*

As the crowd that he and Billie had spent so much effort enticing at their SweetSixteenSalsaSex event started pressing further in about them, Draff's mind froze in wonder at the strength of the smell of the crowd's ardor and expectation. *Perhaps*, he thought with an awakening grin, *they think I'm calling out in anxious passion. I am, aren't I?*

Their experience at this point proved exactly as he and Billie had imagined in their wildest dreams. Almost exactly. Well, perhaps, in truth, more than inexactly. Draff had noticed the lone Enforcer in the distance slipping through the electrified crowd, pushing aside two particularly awe-struck girls. The faceless Enforcer directed its dark opaque face mask first at Billie, then at Draff, who, finally noticing the Enforcer staring fixedly at him, froze and, looking nervously from side-to-side, prepared to run. But even if Draff hadn't noticed, it wouldn't have made any difference. Something suddenly snapped between the three.

Raymond Gaynor

Chapter 24

It didn't require a visual savant to notice Billie's whole body tensing. Draff closed his eyes and reached back, placing his warm, sweaty palms on Billie's muscular hands. Billie, to everyone including Draff's surprise, shook loose and bucked, whinnying like an wild, corralled stallion. Draff, frightened out of his wits, sucked in his breath and hissed a request to Billie to return to their original plan. The crowd, as if thrown into a collective frenzy by Billie's completely unanticipated action, sucked in its collective breath while the two girls continued mimicking Draff and Billie engaged in what everyone assumed was the immediate prelude to actual sex, many on T-Rips imagining they were already engaged in it. *Theirs is the way it was supposed to be,* thought Draff off-handedly. *But this is the way, without our knowing, Billie and my relationship has always seemed fated to go.*

Shaking off everything they had planned and giving in to spontaneity, the two SuperSalsaSexmen faced each other, and, arms flaying, gave up any attempt to embrace in the confusion. *It's all so like my life*, Draff thought, recalling his fourth PerCust, a filler, only there long enough to bridge the six-month gap between the departure of his third, about whom he hated himself for having felt about so strongly physically and emotionally, and his adulthood. Would it have been, was it in fact, the same right now with Billie, given their SweetSixteenSuperSalsaSex event had come to so sudden an abortive end? Standing blankly before Billie and a confused but still wildly expectant crowd, Draff felt as if his heart and body were being presented for purchase in an ancient slave market, suspended as he was in the fire of passion being emitted by his public lover, Billie. Which was it? Love-slave? Lover? Neither? Throughout all their years together, Billie had never abandoned him, or, for that matter, gone mad or died. His relationship with Billie had, up to this moment, argued solidly against everything he feared might happen to Billie if Draff finally, wholeheartedly, let him in. Now it seemed as if the universe, at the last minute, had stepped in between them preventing the inevitabile, conspiring against the future which both had assumed to be theirs.

Like the fifth PerCust? a voice within his head mocked. In truth, during his time with his fourth and fifth PerCusts, Rob actually learned more about himself than he had at any other time in his life. Save perhaps this moment in time and later in his relationship with Simi.

Interesting, Draff thought almost out loud, re-awakening to the fidgeting yet still potentially awestruck, anonymous crowd, which, despite the event's sudden untoward conclusion continued broadcasting its heightened expectations. Billie, a look of unconsummated longing on his face, shivered with unrequited excitement, playing directly to the crowd's prurient delight, while backing slowly, sadly, awkwardly away from Draff, the look of exasperation on his face suggesting he was panicked and about to run. *Interesting how Billie—and Simi for that matter—don't seem to be affected by my "gift" like others*, Draff thought, watching Billie retreat. *On the other hand, had I affected the two girls caricaturing what everyone was expecting, would it have been any different for Billie than what had happened with my previous PerCusts?*

Draff inhaled deeply through his nose, savoring the spicy, randy smell emanating from the crowd, like icing on a tempting cake, covering Billie's metalic scent of fear. Draff outstretched his hands and willed Billie to stop, turn and face him, irrespective of the outcome. A hush descended about the two, each standing tall, momentarily facing the other, eyes ablaze before Billie once again turned and this time ran.

Chapter 25

Draff thought of Simi, asleep, oblivious to the world and his musings. He needed to get going or he'd arrive at Slams so late he would end up having to spend the whole night entertaining, when he already wanted to return home and pick up where he and Simi had left off.

Theirs had proven a particularly serendipitous and, to his mind, unlikely tryst. Draff, after what ended up being one of the most widely publicized, viewed and discussed SweetSixteenSuperSalsaSexcapades of the time, instantly became "Billie's partner." If the two hadn't publicly consummated their desires, it was assumed that they would do so privately soon afterward, and, oh, what a consummation it surely would be, given the publicity their event engendered. Not long after their solar-system-wide holovised event, they took to appearing regularly in public together, hand-in-hand, smiling at each other suggestively, to rousing accolades by passersby and the millions of viewers holographically following their every move and gesture. In fact, their coming out display had garnered Draff not only his mob and group's undivided adoration, but also NewTerran as well as extra-terrestrial fame, translating for Draff into an infinite waiting list of clients at Slams. And there, of course, was the problem: Clearly, Billie still desired him, but Draff, whenever engaged in actual *thoughts* of sex with Billie viewed him more like his third PerCust, a cherished mentor whom he had so liked. Draff would eidetically recall the scent of the intriguing, 30-year-old, native American spiritualist-healer whom he'd driven mad, and begin re-experiencing the unforgettable moments of dissonance. Was the situation the same—in this case substituting Billie for his third PerCust, the result having yet to eventuate? Or, were Billie—and Simi for that matter—so different, so unique from all the other people in the universe, somehow resistant or impervious to whatever curse it was that followed him? Had the government known there was something special about the three back then, and pre-arranged their meeting? Or was it he, this time, who was fated to fall into madness for allowing himself to feel the lust he had harbored for Billie?

That was the circumstances the day that, while Billie was away partying with his growing social circle of gay male friends, Simi had, for no apparent reason, appeared outside the back door of Slams which Draff typically used to exit to avoid any hang-on clients. It was dark. Everything about them seemed as if painted a slick, reflective black after a drenching rain. The alley smelled of half-digested food, moldy clothes and cooling hot asphalt. Alleys, like this one, were all that was left of the highways of yesteryear that had not been converted to pedestrian corridors, and they were fast disappearing.

A momentary waft of jasmine caressed Draff's nostrils, quickly turning into biting sourness. Simi, naked, her normally pale skin ashen in the reflective darkness, looked...downtrodden...worse, downtrodden and desperate. As soon as the heavy stage door clanged shut behind Draff, Simi, a frozen, vaporous ghost, startled, ran directly into his arms and clutched him tightly.

Draff held her until he felt her take a deep, sniffling breath, and her rigid, shaking body relax. For a moment, he worried she might pass out and slip through his embrace onto the wet, stinking pavement. But she didn't. Instead she clutched him tighter and melted through the skin of his monomolecular Flack and the shimmering blue Eugitor he was wearing to press directly against his flesh.

"What is it, Simi?" Draff asked, freeing a hand to stroke her wetted cheek and brush aside a matted wisp of tear-soaked hair. "What's wrong," he whispered softly, his suit growing ruddier wherever they touched.

"C...Correth," was all that she could muster from

her strained, and in Draff's eyes, soft, perfectly formed lips. "Correth," she repeated between sobs digging her fingers into Draff's skin.

Correth, Draff knew, was Simi's newest *almost* lover; the latest in an unending string of girlfriends and almost lovers. He'd met her once. Somewhere. A party perhaps, but just in passing. There was something about the woman that had disturbed him.

"Gone," Simi whispered harshly, out of breath between sobs, eyes welling, releasing more tears. "Oh, Draff. Earlier today we were together…then…" Simi made a noise with her lips as if kissing a lover goodbye. "Why, Draff, why?" she whined, burying her face in his chest to hide the shame he smelled emanating from her. "Why can't I…" her voice trailed off, the sobbing returning.

Completely disarmed, Draff simply repeated, "Why can't you…?"

Draff drew in another breath, noting that, immediately after his reply, her fragrance had changed from sourness back to sweet jasmine then to heady honeysuckle. Looking down at the perfect, curvaceous, feminine creature clutching desperately to him, pleading…for what? Support? Solace? Empathy? His own troubled life had left him with plenty of that. Caring? He had always cared about Simi, after all he, Billie and Simi had always been *the mob*. Family-style affection? Simi, Draff had long ago decided, cared deeply (and hopelessly in his mind) for Billie, who, while Billie was always there for her as a close *friend*, had other affectations. Love? It smelled and felt like that was what she was searching for, yet, even the remotest thought of love—especially physical love—between Draff and her had always seemed incongruous, given her strong, singular, and very public interest in Billie.

Simi stopped crying long enough to look up into Draff's luminous green eyes, made even more intense by the pink, increasingly ruddy glow of his Eugitor. *If Billie is a lizard, Draff is the lizard king*, she thought, sniffling, *searching for something that he knows he wants but doesn't yet recognize. Look down at me, Draff,* she willed. *Look into my eyes. Please.* Draff, as if compelled, shifted his gaze from her warmly inviting body thrust skin-to-skin against him, to the two, sparkling, liquid brown eyes staring up at him. Eyes longingly searching his. The tips of her eyelashes brushed against his neck inviting him to *please* take the next step. *But what?*

For what? Draff's brain quizzed anxiously. "Simi, I..." he began.

Simi clutched him tighter. "Shh," she whispered, sliding her delicate fingers down his chest, entwining hers with his.

Locked together in an ethereal dream, Simi stretched onto her toes, touched her lips to his, her agile tongue tickling the inside of Draff's mouth sampling his masculine crispness. Here was a "real" man—courageous, frank, heroic—caring not just for himself or what other's thought of him, but of everyone about him. *Everyone. Including me.* She tasted him again, slipping the tip of her tongue deeper.

He tasted of more than exquisite manliness. She drew in a breath, savoring his astringent woodsy smell, her fingers and toes curling of their own volition. In the muscular arms encircling and stroking her, she felt an openness and fearlessness for which she had longed her entire life, and knew in that moment that he was the one—in so many ways opposite but equal—for whom she'd been searching. That and infinitely more. His was the one for which her incomplete soul had been searching through time and space. Beyond her present life. Over the centuries. No man or woman had ever made her feel this way; no one, not even Correth, who she was now glad had left her, paving the way for this singularly important moment.

Draff caught himself taken aback. How long had time just stood still? A second? A minute? An hour within the powerful, unfathomable rip in reality that Simi's kiss had somehow called into existence? It wasn't the same with Billie. He and Billie were like toy boats bobbing along on an endless stream, subject to every whim, ripple and wave. Simi was different. *Really* different. It seemed to Draff as if she had indeed just manipulated the fabric of chaotic space-time, and somehow bent it to her will. *Seemed,* or, Draff wondered, *had she actually...?* Thinking back, he recalled a momentary, sharp metallic odor just before it had happened.

To his utter surprise, Draff realized that his Eugitor and Flack were gone—QTransed?—leaving the two in each other's naked embrace in the dark alley. *Had he intentionally slipped out of them in the lost moment or had she actually...?*

Simi knew that Draff would have to see, taste, hear and feel her all at the same time. It wouldn't be enough to smell her naturally-alluring feminine fragrence. He needed to *believe* what he had just and was still experiencing. Draff may have his "special ability," but no one had ever questioned if she might have one of her own.

Simi smiled, pleased with the result, and rubbed her body against his. Draff, to her surprise, tried to gently extricate himself, pressing a palm shakily against her bare shoulder. *He's not accepting what he's experiencing,* Simi thought, once again locking eyes with Draff's. Even so, she could tell from the widening of his jet-black pupils, the heat issuing from his hand on her shoulder, the rise in his heart rate, that his body was acquiescing to the seductive maelstrom raging inside both of them.

Draff slid his hand from Simi's shoulder, gliding his fingertips along the length of her arm to her shivering hand, this time entwining *his* fingers in hers. Never taking her eyes from him, her face softened, and she allowed the promise of a smile to light her face. Eyes widening, she grasped Draff's fingers firmly in hers, tossed her head, rose on her toes and kissed him again.

Draff let himself drift in her wake. He no longer had any idea where he, he and Simi, or for that matter he, she and Billie were proceeding. He felt confused, like a guest passed from person to person at an ancient Roman orgy with nothing solid upon which to grasp. *It was totally different with Billie,* Draff thought. Jackson, the Simi thrusting her body against him, begging him to take her—oh, yes, that was what she was doing; his nose never failed—was so different from the playmate and later, adolescent friend he had known, he was paralyzed. His hands, his lips, his body, however, knew what to do, and immediately began to follow an unconscious, imprinted, primeval set of instincts, leaving him to wonder from where the magnetic energy Simi was clearly spinning about them was coming.

He caressed her cheek, her shoulder, her lips, feeling himself free-falling from a precipice of erotic excitement into a bottomless well of sexual lust. And lust for her, he did. Unremittingly, insatiably, as he had never lusted for anyone before. Not even with Billie during their...

"Yes," she breathed, raising his fingers and wetting their tips with her tongue. "Yes," she whispered, verbalizing her interest, stating clearly her resolve.

Simi slid Draff's wetted fingertips down until they brushed her nether curls and began rocking back and forth against them. Draff reflexively curved his fingertips and Simi began shuddering, digging fingernails into his hardening muscles, moaning and arching. As if on cue, she thrust her hips against his hand, the sides of her milky abdomen flushing scarlet as if just for him.

"Jackson!" Draff began to say, as he felt her body shudder, knowing as he spoke that he would never again be entirely free of her seductive allure. The truth, established in that moment, was that he would never want to.

Simi smiled dreamily, her unfocused eyes dilating. *This is the one*, a distant voice whispered in the back of her head, echoing as it wove its way to the center of her conscious being, along the way joined by one after another distant voice. It was as if every female descendent from her ancestral past were adding its ghostly assent as the voice now working its way from her center throughout her whole body. *This is the one*, they chorused together, their spectral shout creating a misty corporeal glow about the two stunned lovers.

Is this what love feels like? Draff's overwhelmed mind, pressed. *Real love? Beyond the reach of the curse...*

Simi, a look of aghast spreading across her face as she awoke from the other-worldly summons by the voices that had just cast a life-path for the two of them, one that placed her and all her vulnerabilities totally, completely into the hands of this young man towering over her. Whining softly, she began to struggle.

"Whoa...wait..." Draff began, but the look of fear in Simi's glassy eyes told him she was elsewhere, fighting for something that he, in this world, couldn't hope to comprehend. Draff slowly, carefully positioned her upright. Folding her thusting arms over her naked breasts, she seemed to Draff to become like a rag doll, as if the boundless energy she had unleashed had been completely spent.

Cradling her body in his arms, Draff bent awkwardly and picked up the Eugitor and Flack lying at his feet. "Simi, it's okay. Here," he said offering his Flack to her, trying to reassure her of his own desire and willful participation, while at the same time absolving her of what he took for exhaustion and guilt over orchestrating what had just transpired. *She is beautiful, in a truly unworldly way,* he thought. "Simi, it's okay," he repeated contritely, then, "Simi!"

All the fears—hers and those of the chorus of voices both encouraging and at the same time forewarning her—dissolved into general disbelief. Simi opened her eyes and stared blankly at the naked man holding her, her bloodless hands drifting from her breasts towards her mouth as if to scream.

Jackson! What have I done? thought Draff, Simi's look of what could only be terror gripping him in its iron-like vice. Was the sudden change in her a manifestation of the madness people seemed to fall into whenever he allowed them in? Whenever he allowed himself to feel and accept love? Panicked, he reached out, pried her icy hands from her mouth, kissing them warmly, softly, lovingly. *Please, no,* he pleaded, willing her to prove his fear was nothing more.

She didn't resist. A flicker of recognition passed across her face, then it drained of blood, her eyelids fluttered, her eyes rolled and she collapsed in his carrying embrace.

What have I done? What have I done? Brie's mind repeated like a broken record player as he clutched her seemingly lifeless body against him. *But no, she isn't lifeless*, his body assured him. Though barely, she was breathing. He placed his lips next to hers. She was indeed alive, her scent reassured him. Quite alive, and to his amazement, underneath, excited and invitingly receptive.

Draff, knelt and held her tighter, an unspoken admonition

burning his ears: *Protect her. Protect her. Protect her with your life.*

In the pit of his stomach, he had the feeling that he'd botched everything, like he and Billie had their SweetSixteenSalsaSex event, though in fact, he couldn't quite put a mental finger on what the "everything" meant.

He felt her wrist. Her pulse was weak and fast. His nose had assured him correctly that she was alive. That meant it was also likely correct in revealing to him her continued desire.

Draff brushed her hair from her ashen face and wiped a sheen of cold sweat from her brow. The Simi in his arms was of this world, but still eerily half in another. His mind, running at break-neck speed, pressed him, trying to instill the thought that in his arms might be the answer to all his questions: his unusual gift; it's apparently devastating effect on others; the appearance of the idiot-savant girl; the vague disquiet he still felt over the aborted SweetSixteenSalsaSex event with Billie; and now Simi's out-of-nowhere crazy behavior. He draped her with his Flack and Eugitor, stood upright and began carrying her back to her nest, shaking his head as he went in disbelief. The world was more than mad, it was yet again changing beneath, around, and within him even as it was unfolding about him, and where it was going in its rush was anyone's guess.

Chapter 26

When NewAmerican adolescents come into their SweetSixteen, they are no longer required to have a PerCust or remain within their contracted social family. For the first time in his life, Draff Rob Brie [Septican-Smite]'s life was entirely his own. Unisensory savants his last custodian had explained towards the end of their time together, usually remained such throughout their life struggling with deficits in their other senses not infrequently in inverse proportion to the extent of their gift. A few would eventually develop into synesthetic savants—individuals who could somehow successfully meld one, two, three or, in the rarest of cases, all of their senses with their primary sensory gift. In such cases, the state kept a close eye on the "mutant" because government Artificial Intelligence programs (ArtFarts in NewSpeak) had trouble predicting their behavior. If synesthesia happened, what typically resulted was a person who could, for example, "see" taste, "feel" colors, "taste" another's touch and "smell" the color of a sunrise. *Any* combination, of course, was possible. Rob's special sense of smell was already beckoning him on towards new, uncharted sensory territory, ramping up as if anticipating synesthesia.

Sometimes synesthesia led to unmeasurable genius. Rob's last PerCust had thought it possible that he, Rob, might be a latent meta-genius assuming the mental cost of reinterpreting, assimilating, reconnecting and containing all the hyper-sensory information he would have to deal with didn't entirely overwhelm him. That was the PerCust's theory —and hope—which Rob was grasping tightly onto these days.

It didn't generally go that well for synesthetes. Most would remain unisensory, some denying their gift, relegating it to semi- or unconsciousness. For them, their "gift" was at best an inconvenient nuisance, at worse a dis-ease wanting a cure. Others fought their way to fuller consciousness while refusing the gift outright. The loneliness and isolation accompanying this approach inevitably consumed most of their psychic energy, fighting their talent and, as a consequence, their own self. A few would end up frankly psychotic, especially if their ability, as in Rob's case, was unusual in some way; in a worst case scenario these few would end being socially reviled as dark or evil. Society, in attempting to "help" such persons with experimental treatments, would often end up medicating or damaging them out of conscious existence. In such cases, the savant often ended up being spiritually exorcised or surgically altered and, again, ultimately destroyed. A remaining handful would end up criminally abusing their "gift" for personal comp.

The real outliers, like Brie and the idiot girl savant, would struggle to integrate their specialness, at the same time accepting the accompanying fear, not so much of the gift, as of themselves. Rob empathized most easily with this point-of-view, and continued applying his gift to further explore himself and the world in his own increasingly unique way. It was a case of the programmer no longer being able to fully understand his own programs. The result was that the more he attempted to use his gift, the more he attempted to hide it from everyone except his closest friends while remaining exquisitely sensitive to physical, social, psychic or spiritual side effects it might cause in others. And, of course, himself. The program, so to speak was now programming itself in ways so unusual that no one, including the programmed, could understand it. In the process, he was slowly being granted a new perspective on life, watching himself as if from above at a close but emotionally-detached distance, while his ability grew, matured and expanded in discrimination and power. Others may not know or struggle with such a burden, but he knew in his heart, mind, and yes, soul that either because of the gift or his acceptance of it, he had an appointment with destiny. It was this thought more than any other that allowed him to walk around rather than through the many other pitfalls into which sensory savants typically fell.

At SweetSixteen, Rob was ready to reach out on his own, and reach he did...for Billie, and he still felt the pull even after their less-than-successful (in their minds) but publicly awesome (in everyone in the universe else's minds) SweetSixteenSalsaSexcapade.

Billie, at the same time, found himself having to repeatedly let go of Brie, only recently coming into his own understanding of himself, his pros and cons. Though, at the moment, his future seemed, or he wanted it to seem, still interwoven tightly with Draff's, he knew better. Irrespective of how the event had unfolded in reality and in their minds, they both had to acknowledge that they "fit" well together. They were a couple—they had been since childhood—though their coupling had now taken on a decidedly maturer bent. Put more simply, Billie continued to lust for Draff, while Draff, despite his widening interests, still yearned for Billie's...companionship.

Billie's tack worked, from his point of view, too well. Draff, having partially let go, was no longer aware on a moment-to-moment basis of Billie's lust, though he frequently welcomed it, much to Billie's delight and equal consternation. It was, nonetheless obvious to everyone in their group that Billie yearned—physically ached—for

Draff, while Draff, on the other hand, was busy refocusing his awareness on Billie's newly developed, wildly potent and virile odor in the presence of *other* men, especially gay men, who were equally interested coupling with either of the two.

Whenever, out of curiosity, Billie asked Draff what it was exactly that he smelled when around him, Draff caught himself doing his best to avoid an honest answer. Draff, whenever around Billie, was becoming increasingly aware of a newly developing feeling inside of both of them. Call it envy or jealousy or simply unrequited lust. Ever since their SweetSixteenSalsaSexcapade, Draff could smell the same new, underlying tang in both their scents.

Immediately after the event, Draff had asked, "Ah. How are you?" while staring at the naked man standing before him in what later would become an oft replayed personal ritual between the two.

"Fine. You?" Billie had answered and would answer, catching his breath.

"Good. I…I think we did okay," Draff had proffered and would proffer weakly, the crowd and later anyone near them hanging on their every word.

"Yeah, me, too," Billie had countered and would continue to counter with a shy but wry smile on his face. During their SweetSixteenSalsaSexcapade, several in the crowd about them mimicked his knowing smile; as later, anyone happening to be near enough to them would do. In the end neither said what he really wanted to say, perhaps because neither really knew. Not then or even now.

For Draff, their event was all about smell. Thinking back, the crowd's scent hadn't actually been a strict recombination of individual odors, like garlic, coffee, or vanilla mixed together. The collective sum wasn't like anything that he'd ever smelled before. Yet, there they were, each person's unique, unmistakable, individual olfactory signature, tinged by that person's immediate emotional or empathetical state, but the whole, something more. Something almost alive. *The catalyst*, Draff analyzed, *must be the overall group's emotional state. And where emotions are involved, it is all about subtle, moment-to-moment changing nuances. Perhaps that's why it seemed alive.*

His last PerCust would have tried to tease them out into individual "pheromonal signatures," for most people, strongly emotional and evocative reflexively off-gas pheromones though completely unconsciously. To Brie, their scent and their individual pheromonal signatures were both there, separately, and yet, together the two somehow broadcast an additional meta-component. Draff and Billie's SweetSixteenSalsaSexcapade was providing Draff an opportunity to explore what he was coming to think of as igneous-like chemical emotions: vague, subtle, volatile in the gaseous sense, incredibly informative to those who could sense them, and always in-the-face powerful.

Another of his PerCusts had briefly pointed out that a woman's menstrual period would typically synchronize to another's just from the two being near enough to smell each's scent, allowing the more socially dominant to "control" the other's menstrual timing. As proof, their synchronized periods could be easily disrupted simply by the presence of a virile male. For almost everyone except Draff, this phenomenon was completely unconscious, more like a bias that pushed each individual to enact certain behaviors. Nonetheless, a person's life could be totally changed from merely one such unconscious event. For Draff, however, it was a million times more. So much so, he was convinced, that in the act of being conscious of it, Draff could, in turn, subtly but powerfully change the "normal" person's thoughts and behavior. Earlier he had theorized that this might be how he was affecting the kind of changes he had so guiltily observed in his PerCusts. *But it can't be that,* he reminded himself in frustration, *because I am as aware of any change in their as I am in my own smell, and while theirs changed, mine didn't seem to...*

In fact, post-event, Billie hadn't gone mad (though admittedly his signature had become more "mature"—

more "adult" and to some extent, unstable) and as it did, another concern began nagging at the back of Draff's mind: that like his past five adult custodians, like the menstrating girls in the experiment he had read about, Billie, by simply by being around him, might have been changed, and that change would usher in the end of their relationship. Perhaps Billie would come to "respect" him while ultimately rejecting him. If that were to happen, he, Draff, should be able to tell by comparing his recollection of his and Billie's immediate pre-SweetSixteen odor signatures with those when together now. Everything he'd heard in the past suggested his gift of smell, and the consequences of acknowledging and nurturing it, shouldn't in and of itself be able to cause such a change in others, but, every day his ability, discrimination, and the pull to act based on smell, should grow stronger. And it did.

Perhaps, Draff thought, *it would have happened anyway.* Billie had been lovingly tolerant and supportive of Draff's very exhibitionistic con. It was Draff's particular pro that Billie found unavoidably intriguing and that Draff had become quite adept at working during his years of con at Slams. Draff, in fact, delighted playing to a crowd while inwardly fully experiencing and yet somehow insulating himself from their combined feelings, an addictive combination for which he had become famous at Slams and which he had repeatedly demonstrated at his and Billie's SweetSixteenSalsaSexcapade. It would be many years before people stopped talking about their public coming-of-age event, and even more he suspected before he would fully understand the depth and breadth of all that transpired that night.

One constant, however, that was inherently pleasing to Draff was the place they'd chosen to stage their public exhibition. To the businesses nearby, it had provided a huge, captive audience to whom to whisper business advertisements.

Advertisement programs, typically in sleep mode, when sensing excitement in a crowd, would immediately switch into active mode, in this particular location, initiating sexually-laced sales algorithms that would not just play to, but enhance each person's most erotic, most potentially heavily draining sexual fantasies. Take that into account, and Draff and Billie's appearance, despite the actual outcome, resulted in nearby retailers resolutely hyping every possible aspect of the event including offering clothes similar to those the couple had doffed, their jewelry, body marks, makeup, even the style and color of their head, pubic and body hair, including Draff's TARS-AID prehensile tail, as well as any props or other proprietary add-ons, whether pre-planned or serendipitously appearing at the event. The BOPIS wholesale merchandiser's idea was to lure customers to spontaneously purchase high-drain items which they could presumably use to re-experience the event again later, at that same time associating the resulting thrill with that particular business.

Draff had became aware of the Enforcer, only when it was standing directly in front of him, the front of one of its hobnail boots pressing against the smallest of Draff's naked toes. The sudden realization had caused him to freeze. Draff reflexively splayed all ten digits to steady himself as Billie gyrated to the earth-shaking rhythm of the song they had chosen for just this moment, the song which Billie, thank Jackson, had retained just enough presence to remember to turn on with a flick of his wrist at exactly the right moment.

While the music continued to hammer out its barbaric beat, the crowd, transformed into a mass of rhythmically undulating primitives, began bobbing their heads and bodies, hooting in ape-like unison to the savage, increasingly rude strains of music. As quickly as it began, the magic that had catapulted Draff, Billie and the crowd into a realm high above where their physical bodies were rocking in ecstatic unison had begun dissolving.

Naked, Draff, who had stood facing his eager young partner surrounded by innumerable gawking strangers intent on catching every detail of the spectacle, shuddered at the

Enforcer's presence while Billie tensed and prepared to run.

Raymond Gaynor

Chapter 27

Only during SweetSixteen were youth like Draff and Billie permitted by the government to plan and execute a SalsaSexcapade. This was, in essence, an opportunity for the government and its citizens to openly acknowledge and ultimately de-secretize sex. The only objection was that, due to their popularity, really popular events like Draff and Billie's could sometimes cause significant disruption.

When NewAmerica began critically re-examining its failing infrastructure, social investigators—SoGators in NewSpeak, rational observers rather than scientists who looked for repetitious processes and events with always the same outcome—began analyzing the "messages" underlying announcements issued by the government, business, and collective society. Private business announcements, or "b-casts," were examined first, followed by "g-casts" or governmental announcements primarily regarding newly enacted laws or regulations, followed then by "t-casts"—personal social posts. The result was universal horror when it became obvious that b-casts to which public as a whole were constantly being bombarded, were, by their nature, rife with violence. More horrifying, however, was the subsequent realization that b-casting was an unconscious harbinger of violence and chaos—expressed in a form of ubiquitous lawlessness—which, when politicized, translated to a constant call to anarchy with intent destroy the fabric of the very society that was allowing, even eulogizing, the "right" to b-cast. B-casting had many aliases in the pre-Jacksonian years: marketing and advertising were two of the commonest. The point was to alter the receiver's behavior, and the key was to come up with a way to bypass consumer volition. As a result, protesters of this subtle but admittedly violational form of messaging became popular heroes, dissenting without providing any viable alternatives, in essence, sanctifying public negativity, violence and chaos. At the same time, there was no way for anyone, young or old, to learn about and promote the most important and instinctive societally-binding impulses of humans: empathy, cooperation, affection, that that made government and society actually work. In popular terms, non-violent, volitional acts, the quinessence of which was sex. Jacksonian society in a knee-jerk reaction turned to SalsaSex as the answer.

Even so, SalsaSex didn't come into being solely as the result of socio-investigative reflection surrounding b-casting, but rather also from the heated public discussions that resulted when the results and implications of b-casting were made known. Public sentiment, influenced by a tsunami of defensive b-, g- and t-caster op-eds, quickly divided into two "camps," either "for" or "against" violence. In the end, SweetSixteenSalsaSex was born of the group at the center of the "problem"—the millions identifying themselves as victims of violation: namely, the adolescent youth of NewAmerica. What surprised everyone was that by permitting and encouraging flagrantly youthful sex in public, it quickly came to represent the fundamental ideal that society had been hopelessly struggling to *appropriately* implement: Sex education had, for the first time, actually been initiated *by the public for its own pleasure and edification.* Best of all, the solution caught on like wildfire and actually worked.

These public "events" proved to be, in the fullest sense of their meaning, *events,* replete with sub-events, some governmental, some private, some social, others spontaneously spectator- generated. During Draff and Billie's event, the young woman on Draff's far left was broadcasting her desire and immediate willingness to rut with two unesconsed young men at the front of the crowd who were cradling each other lovingly within what to her was undoubtedly her own remembered or imaginary male lover's arms. At the same time, the man standing immediately next to her—obviously her current mate—issued a vague, barely perceptible scent that reminded Draff more of a eunuch. Clearly, something had long since gone awry for the two, and the feelings they once held each had significantly diminished.

An elderly couple behind them, tears streaking both's cheeks, were no doubt remembering their own youthfully uninhibited pairings. Draff could smell it clearly, and the fear of the effect he assumed he must be asserting this moment on these onlookers and on Billie returned, washing away whatever bliss to which Draff had so looked forward. *Brown,* Draff cursed silently in the extreme, aware that bliss was exactly what the crowd was hungering for, more so even than the actual consummation of two young men's thus far unrequited sex.

Two adolescent boys had stood, hand-in-hand, staring awestruck at Draff and Billie from behind the sad couple whose partial life story Draff had both surreptitiously and quite unwillingly read through their smell. The boys were having an entirely different experience. Smiling mischievously at one another, each turned and searched the other's eyes. Draff smiled, wondering what their SweetSixteenSalsaSexcapade would be like. Unlike Draff and Billie, these two had a long, interesting and fulfilling journey ahead together. He could smell it.

An elderly man and woman further to the left, also holding hands, eyes riveted on Draff, seemed to be trying to make sense out of the two naked young men seemingly at the knife-edge of and fully prepared for but oddly not engaged in sex. The woman shook her head as if thinking sadly, *What's happening to our world; what have today's children become?* But the twinkle in her eyes and her smell betrayed her well-hidden but continued desire to once again experience wild, unbridled sex with the elderly man beside her. *Just once more*, her scent pleaded. Just once more with the oblivious man beside her. *Once more before we pass from this earth.* They both projected an over-smell of immanent death, but in grand form, the woman smiled warmly at the ancient-looking man hunched beside her and squeezed his hand lovingly.

To Draff's surprise, squatting immediately behind Billie, at Draff's eye level, her eyes searching his, was the idiot-savant who had made such an indelible impression on him, obvious not only by her familiar olfactory signature, but also from its new, ripe, maiden aroma and the co-presence of her disgruntled custodian gripping her hand and trying to pull her away. A waft off the old man's sweaty hand passed near enough to Draff to cause Draff's nose to wrinkle and his face to grimace. The old man smelled of lasciviousness. Pure carnal lust. It was plain to Draff in that instant, the girl's custodian wanted her for himself. It was equally plain to Draff that she had no interest whatsoever in him, and was prepared to fight him off (again and again) if necessary. The situation was one rife for violence, the kind that, should it be acted out, would likely cause her a lifetime of hurt and pain. Draff's heart opened to her. Yet, standing next to Billie, Draff could only sigh, a gesture both Billie and the crowd took to represent romantic desire and satisfaction, to which the crowd spontaneously began to applaud.

Draff Rob Brie [Septican-Smite] awkwardly returned her gaze. There was something unsettling about the girl, now a fecund young woman and, quite likely Draff predicted from her past actions and current demeanor, while not necessarily highly intelligent she was quite clever. Her dark, reddish-brown hair, speckled hazel eyes and striking opalescent skin reminded him of what little he could recall of his own bio-em. And of Simi.

Draff tore his eyes from the girl, in the process catching a fleeting glimpse of a barely perceptible, off-center smile she was obviously directing at him and him alone. Shifting his gaze back to Billie, he was surprised to see Billie staring over a shoulder, wide-eyed, directly at the girl.

What the Jackson? thought Draff, standing further upright. Billie didn't notice. The girl and most of the onlooker's attention was riveted not on either the girl or Billie and his all too masculine body, but to Draff's reaction of surprise. To Draff's dismay, the idiot-girl pointed at his nakedness and joined in with the two giggling girls, located just behind the unmoving enforcer in front and to his side.

Draff's face flushed, the redness spreading from face to chest to thighs to toes until his entire body glowed the same color as his flaming curls. Smiling awkwardly, he began searching for the clothes he'd shed at the start of what was quickly becoming in his mind a complete fiasco. Squatting to slip back into them, he searched through the many feet around him, eventually noting Billie, who, after returning his gaze momentarily to Draff, had turned and run.

Chapter 28

This is my *SalsaSex party!* My *SweetSixteen!* My *FLIC! Nobody can take that away from me!* Draff desperately tried to reassure himself, steeling his body as he stood tall and, after looking in the direction of his fleeing partner, turned to face the crowd that, assuming this was part of the event, pressed hungrily for whatever came next. Reaching out with his hands and inwardly with his feelings, Draff summoned all the love and affection he had for Billie, placed his arms around a phantom Billie's neck and kissed the air passionately.

The audience responded, imaging the illusory Billie, stunned, then smile diffidently with joy, scooping Draff into his arms and carrying him away. The young woman, flagrantly broadcasting her desire to the two supposedly gay young men, was by now rutting openly with both, her mate looking on longingly. The elderly couple, remembering their own youthfully uninhibited pairings, were snuggling in a lover's embrace. The two mischievous boys locked hands and offered the other a giddy first kiss. The ancient looking man grinned from ear-to-ear, returned his wife's hand squeeze. The two giggling girls, at first staring uncomprehendingly, joined hands and disappeared into the crowd. Only the idiot-girl refused to be drawn into the mass delusion. Nose in the air, she turned and walked away, her lecherous custodian following like a lapdog. The Enforcer alone remained unmoving, silent, cold and faceless.

What the Brown? Draff replayed in his mind, imagining Billie, in blissful reverie, closing his eyes, and returning the kiss. Draff parted his lips to receive the kiss and lost himself in the illusion of the moment...

Chapter 29

A gentle tap at his elbow brought Draff back. The crowd had dissipated and late night shoppers eager to pick up their wares were rushing about ignoring the two naked boys, Draff and Billie staring at each other, ignoring the surging throngs. The thousands of whispers coursing about the two created a briefly lingering aural space within which the two, still wanting desperately to enact their passions, were quickly replaced by the busy click and scrape of heels passing on the pavement. Only the faceless Enforcer remained, standing motionlessly beside them, holding in one hand Draff's and in the other Billie's clothes. Draff stared into the opaque mask and sniffed discretely without success. The statue before them continued holding out their clothes while maintaining its fixed, silent stance.

Draff and Billie simultaneously reached for the clothes and receiving them, nervously began to redress, Draff scanning the passing crowd for any sign of the idiot-girl, and Billie, following his lead, searching the same crowd. *For what?* Draff wondered. *For whom?* his mind added with marked irritation. Was he looking for same girl Draff was, and if so, why? What interest could Billie possibly have in her? Billie was gay. Solidly. Completely. Totally. At least according to Billie. So why would he take an interest in a girl, especially this one? Was there some reason known only to Billie that she appeared at this particular time and at this particular spot? Or was serendipity once again at work stirring the pot? Draff, not spotting her or her goosebump-raising custodian in the flood of people passing them or in the distant night shadows, realized with a jolt that his thoughts were initiating jealously. *Why would I be jealous about—or was it of—either this girl or Billie?*

It surprised, then hurt Draff to have to acknowledge that a well of jealousy did, in fact, exist within him. *Love is the Jacksonist thing,* he thought, shaking his head to clear the many conflicting rogue thoughts competing for his attention. Slipping a hand into Billie's, he stared at Billie's face. It was glowing with confidence, accompanied by an equally unexpected yearning welling from somewhere within Draff. *I want him*, Draff admitted grudgingly. *I want him and I want him to myself.* The statement echoed back and forth within his reeling mind. *Yes, but why—and why so desperately? And what is it behind what I'm feeling? Love? Desire? Devotion? Friendship?*

Draff and Billie, shifted side-by side and dressed

silently, each lost in his thoughts, the Enforcer remaining unchanged, unmoving, its extended but now vacant arms outstretched like a robot in sleep mode. As soon as they'd finished, Draff nervously nudged Billie and they walked off together, each looking repeatedly back over his shoulder at the still motionless, but slowly receding Enforcer. Draff squeezed Billie's hand and rubbed his other playfully against Billie's shoulder while the enigmatic Enforcer disappeared into darkness as if he had never been. It felt good to be away from it...him...it. There was something frighteningly strange about Enforcers, especially this one, and the entity that must reside inside all that protective gear. But for Draff, it wasn't its look. It was its smell, for the entity inside consistently emanated none at all.

Raymond Gaynor

Chapter 30

Having completed their SweetSixteenSalsaSexcapade and formal studies, Draff and Billie, now a public celebrity *au pair,* reluctantly left the expansive yet familiar nest that had been the center of their social lives for so long to accept an invitation from Remi Edward Alex [Corsi-Mant], a friend of Billies and a rising T-rip programmer, to join him in an all-adult foray. Joining a foray meant living in a shared group flat—a young adult "commune"—to which they would commit a regular percentage of their sally in return for social support and protection. A foray carried with the merry-making a sense of adult responsibility, each member's responsibility being to explore and redevelop a new network, this time of adult friendships, affections and sexual liaisons. A successful SweetSixteenSalsaSex event was the key needed to open the door to the best forays, and Draff and Billie's event was universally regarded as one of the most successful ever. Relationships that formed within forays were expected to last a lifetime. For adults, the foray was the principal social unit of post-Jacksonian

NewAmerica. For Draff, it meant letting go of his former mob and his mob/group leadership role, requiring him to refocus instead on melding into another's, in this case Edward's, social foray.

The building they moved into was a flamboyant, 200th floor, 1950's retro-style, *art nouveau* penthouse that overlooked the entirety of *Chica Centro* just above the rinse-line. On a usual day, the domicile's 30-foot tall, 360-degree, circular floor-to-ceiling window framed a boundless carpet of slowly undulating, cotton-like clouds with the tops of thousands of similar buildings poking through. The buildings projecting through the cloud layer blazed in a panoply of garish colors in the harsh, stratospheric sun. Those who could afford to live at this height were blessed by day with nothing less than a panoramic kaleidoscope of colorful modern art, and by night with a horizon-to-horizon black vista awash with diamond-studded stars. The perpetually romantic ambiance re-stirred within both Brie and Billie the mutual affection they had pledged each other before their famously infamous SweetSixteenSuperSalsaSextravaganza.

Several weeks after moving in, Simi was invited by Edward to join the foray, to which she happily agreed. For her, it was a dream come true. Her pre-SweetSixteen group had proven less than ideal, more competitive than cooperative, tagging her as a nosey little smart-ass, relegating her to the fringe. As a result, Simi never shook off her need to be constantly on the alert. Her only respite was once again resurrecting the triumvirate she, Draff and Billie had maintained unbroken for so long. Unbroken, that is, until Draff and Billie's SweetSixteenSalsaSex event and their leaving the mob to join Edward's foray. Even so, their mob which had been an island of true friendship in a sea of uncertainty for Simi, was already beginning to wear painfully thin when Billie and Draff began seriously planning their SweetSixteenSalsaSex debut, a debut that to her bitter disappointment hadn't included her directly.

In Edward's foray, she was immediately accorded the full measure of adult respect for which she had so often before literally cried herself to sleep. Simi suspected—and desperately wanted to believe—that Draff and Billie were somehow behind the invitation, but carefully avoided the topic, given their collective newness to adult forayship. Still, just suspecting "her two boys" might have been behind the invitation rekindled her positive feelings for each. The foray members treated Simi, Draff and Billie as a distinct threesome from the moment she joined, and whether in the end their *pas de trois* would survive, she treasured the feeling of belonging. She knew that unlike adolescent mobs and groups, relationships within a foray were supposed to last a lifetime, and this one, with Draff and Billie included, was already taking on all the markings of such. On the other hand, she was also aware that relationships within a foray, especially early ones, were like ocean waves, constantly co-mingling to the point that an early liaison like their threesome would be unlikely to persist and would likely prove irrelevant in the end.

It was during their first months together in their new foray that all three together applied for and registered their adult pros and cons, establishing their respective comps or sally upon which they would rely throughout the rest of their adult life. Simi quickly became the destined world-class acronymeur everyone except her knew she would be. Billie fell into bodywork as naturally as Draff into slamming, and together the three commanded enough sally to live well—*very* well, in fact—and to quickly accrue enough contro to allow them any adaptive reconstructive surgery or ARS that each, as a newly debuted adult, might choose as a physical congener that would serve uniquely identify them.

For Draff, there was always only one ARS in which he had been interested throughout his adolescent life: a prehensile tail—prehensile in the sense of being able to act as a combination fifth arm, fifth leg and eleventh finger. He smiled whenever he thought how it would enhance his professional reputation, giving him something unique enough in the slamming world to be a trademark, maybe even create a unique branding opportunity, something for which all slammers lived.

Surprisingly, Billie was the throwback, constantly investigating ARSs, always intrigued, but never committing to any one. For Billie body modification meant augmenting what he had already acquired through old-fashioned exercise and sweat. Given his strong masculinity, outgoing personality and public predilection, he really didn't see the need for anything more. ARS for Billie was unnatural—more of a puzzle, making those who obtained one a paradox. Among gays, he was already revered, but his antiquated attitude towards ARS more often than not left him odd man out—a rebel, a gorilla amidst gentlemen.

Simi—technically still Andry at this point as she clearly fit into foray but had not yet taken Draff, Billie or anyone else for that matter as a lover—was the mysterious one. She liked to remind everyone that she was a moon-child, ever changing, never the same, and so her choice of ARS seemed to ever vary and never crystalize. In fact, however, there was a new, singular, never-spoken constant in her life: a deep, feral attraction to and at the same time abiding love for Rob—Draff to her ever since their intense commingling at night outside Slams. That "secret" remained hidden, and in living the lie, which everyone actually suspected, it made her seem even more mysterious.

Since their SweetSixteenSalsaSexcapade, everyone inside and outside the foray assumed that Draff and Billie were a couple, well on their way toward becoming life-partners, perhaps well on their way to becoming that rarest and most revered of relationships these days, soul mates. Everyone in the foray also knew that Rob still regarded Andry as Andry, not Simi. Yet, over the next couple weeks what began innocently enough as special "friendly caring" for each other, resulted in an almost religious quest on Andry's part to save Rob from himself by redirecting his sexual attentions and desires back to where she felt they belonged: on a woman. More specifically, her.

The challenge in Andry's mind was not one of proclivity, but rather about how exactly to awaken him to her particular gifts: her own constantly increasing intellect, her bulldog-like determination, her resolute spiritual belief in their destiny together. Andry acknowledged at this point in her life (to herself at least) that while she was neither gay nor a savant, she was special in her own way. She had been abundantly afforded her own "gifts"—both her natural female endowments and talents, alongside the promise of immortality through children—which she felt of equal value compared to either of her compatriot's *fortes*, and absolutely necessary in her mind to counterbalance the utter craziness in which Draff's peculiar talent often seemed to lead him. Her feminine intuition assured her that Rob wasn't fundamentally gay, and time and effort was exactly what Andry felt Rob had unconsciously presented her by inviting her to join Edward's foray. And that was all the justification she needed.

Raymond Gaynor

Chapter 31

Andry's own SweetSixteen debut hadn't been—well, it actually hadn't ever happened. The opportunity slid by unnoticed, partly to her relief and partly to her indignant consternation. Though everyone had a SweetSixteen—a year of coming out, of debuting on the world stage one way or another—not everyone chose to do it in as public and as sensational a way as Draff and Billie. For Andry, her long anticipated SweetSixteen ended up a year of introspection accompanied by inner change. The change, however, wasn't the usual transition from youth to adulthood, or from adolescence to womanhood. For Andry, it was a year of emotional rearrangement that ultimately changed her life in an even more radical way than any SalsaSexcapade extravaganza could have. And it was all about her and Rob, though she suspected and hoped she was the only one who knew it, at least for the moment.

While Draff and Billie were busy boasting, to her mind, like young bucks, about their sexual prowess and more recently what kind of ARS they would choose, Andry was struggling with the totality of her transformation—what amounted to a complete metamorphosis. She didn't favor *any* kind of ARS, though she didn't completely dismiss the idea. She talked with several girlfriends, and whenever possible Rob, sleuthing, probing, trying to uncover anything—including anything ARS—that might somehow open the door to more intimacy and an eventual coupling with Rob. Living in constant close proximity in their common foray, the romantic pull was rapidly becoming an admittedly physical drive: a deep, inexplicable longing of the heart, and more recently, of the body as well.

She and Draff were simply meant to be. Of that she was certain. What continued to frustrate her was finding the cusp, the nexus, the critical moment when opportunity would present and allow destiny to take charge. What frustrated her no end was her constant agonizing over whether she would recognize and thereby be able to seize and act on that moment. More recently, she had begun to worry if she would be able to maintain the vigil long enough for it to finally happen. And then, when it occurred, if her strength and resolve would be sufficient to act as decisively as she intuited would be required.

In her heart, Andry knew she was not just Draff's life or even soul mate. What she knew without reservation was that she was his salvation. She knew it the moment they first met as children. Something very adult, very physical—integral, perfect, consummate—had awakened and begun stirring within her from that moment, and what was awakened had now become a necessary total obsession. She knew for certain that Draff Rob Brie [Septican-Smite] was the missing piece of her future, and she his. He was too young back then to know it or have any concept really of destiny, but *she* knew that both of them were inextricably entwined. That knowledge had been enough to sustain her over the years, enough at least until now.

Andry, to her surprise, was neither jealous of Billie nor Rob's love for him. Neither did she envy Billie. She didn't even feel vengeful for his having led Rob down the tortuous path to their now infamous SweetSixteenSalsaSextravaganza event. She was, if anything, patient. Somehow, someway, someday, Draff would awaken to the fact that she was always there for and beside him—supportive, caring, forbearing, and, yes, loving him without reservation. Starting today, however, she resolved to add to her list of attributes "inviting."

It would be subtle, of course. It would have to be. It wouldn't be right to wish for or contribute in any way to splitting up Draff and Billie. No, that would not get her where she and Draff needed to be. Billie clearly loved Draff, and Draff loved him, in her mind, in a Greek sort of way.

Each provided the other the manly support she knew was necessary at this time in their lives to more fully develop their concept of love—ultimately, in Draff's case between a man and a woman. And she wanted that kind of relationship to last their lifetime. A relationship inured against the indifferent and often malicious vicissitudes of time and events. This she knew in her female heart and mind, though the rest of her didn't—*couldn't* really—understand it, no matter how hard she tried. What was it Draff found in Billie that he couldn't find in greater measure in her?

The story of Draff and Billie's recent SalsaSexcapade was still the talk of the town. It had proven utterly wild, natural (or at least seemingly so), totally romantic, erotic and undeniably sensual. Male or female, hermaphrodite, gay or lesbian, straight, bisexual or asexual, it didn't matter. All agreed that these two were the pinnacle of what every couple should and any couple could ever hope to be.

And yet…what had the two girlfriends of hers who carefully placed themselves at the forefront of the boys' public orgy said about the elderly couple watching? The woman had shaken her head. *Shaken her head*, Andry knew in her heart, *in sad disbelief.* All four women, she felt certain—and Draff somewhere deep inside, too—knew that in spite of it all, something was missing, and it wasn't physical consummation. It was as if a tiny, irritating pebble lay buried beneath the layers of man-man love in which the two boys were wrapping themselves, and upon which they were attempting to build. In her opinion, it was all too perfect, all too idyllic, all too *contrived*. In her mind's eye, she could imagine Draff as Billie's Greek Petroclus, while at the same time each the other's Achilles' heel. Draff, for his part, was a canvas upon which Billie was painting, but the best it could ever be was a greyscale caricature of what *she* could offer him. Rob was simply searching for himself in the wrong arms. His destiny lay in hers, and, with the same certainty of heart, hers in his.

It was during the third week of living in the new foray that the moment for which she had been waiting materialized. It wasn't a sudden event or mystical revelation, a telling dream, a message from some Higher Power. It was yet another slow but powerful internal change that she could feel happening within her. She was coming of age, not just physically and emotionally, but spiritually as well.

For most modern adults, ARSs were both the epitome and the culmination of adolescence, crowning the myriad changes that adolescence inevitably brought with it. For Andry, her ARS took a unique form: that of a deeply *spiritual* transformation. Andry—as the ancient Greek philosopher Socrates had challenged every future generation to do—rediscovered the past—*her* past—and through it herself. A past that had been wholly lost to her during childhood and coming of age in part due to her special education.

"Discovered," however, while smartly descriptive, wasn't entirely the right word. Her past hadn't been conspiratorially hidden or secreted away. She could still vaguely remember her bios, though her social family, custodian, PerCust and mob had always been sufficient for the time. Unlike most products of her time, however, she secretly knew her mother's name.

Her mother was the mythical Amelie Stewart, first mistress of NewAmerica, the woman who somehow bound Jackson's gay political specialists Tripler and Clarke together and helped lead them to usher in the NewTimes. The woman that people today talked of in hushed whispers while standing before thousands of memorials to her all over the world. In some circles, her bio-em was still worshipped as a real Goddess. That is to say as an equal to the holy Tripler, Clark and Jackson trinity. The night after Andry's one year of age party—a year before Amelie Stewart had given her daughter to the child's new social family—Amelie placed a tiny, finely filigreed silver triquestra pendant, incised with a Celtic dolphin, fish and butterfly into the palm of Andry's sho-em. From then, it had always appeared about Andry's neck. Andry had been told by her first sho-em custodian "Jan"—of Andry's first or prime social family, Jan-Rho—

just after her bio-em died later that year, Amelie Stewart had also passed on a secret: The pendant around pretoddler Andry's neck had passed from matriarch to matriarch of the bio-line for over twenty centuries. It represented an ancient Celtic order that had passed into contemporary oblivion like so many other religions when NewAmerica was reforged.

The pendant was a source of constant fascination to baby Andry. Over the years, she imagined it held within it a power as ancient as it's origins, not religious, for religions in NewTimes had evolved into social clubs more like businesses; social clubs based often on beliefs that typically flew against what one might experience in the "real" world. Andry's sho-em, Jan, would later reveal to Andry that she had been told by Amelie Stewart herself that the pendant held within it the power to amplify the spiritual power of the wearer. "It's a good thought, whether true or not," Andry's sho-ef always added.

Andry, the child, neither understood nor cared, yet the pendant was never off her slender neck. Over the years, it became like a familiar reminder of her bios and the love, though unremembered, within which she, Andry, surely must have been brought into the world. As an adolescent, she would imagine it calling to her as if wanting to tell her something. Something important about her and her life. But in the telling, whatever message it might have been trying to convey always vanished before she could understand.

And, though she wasn't supposed to, she also secretly knew the identity of her bio-ef: Adelphous "Addy" Tripler, the famous "Rock of NewAmerica" as ex-President Alexander Mathias "Alexander the Great" Jackson, the iconized architect of NewAmerica, liked to call him. Andry had long surmised that her stubbornness, resiliency, intellect and understanding came from her renowned, outwardly "gay" father.

Aside from inheriting an uncanny resemblance to her bio-em, and several not-so-feminine attributes from her bio-ef, what else she'd inherited from them other than the necklet, remained an unanswered question that had resolutely evaded her up. Up to now. The answer, blazing bright in her mind, spiraling inward like the yellow brick road in her favorite bedtime story, *The Wizard of Oz* now lay open before her: She had come to realize, or perhaps more accurately *decided*, that she had inherited the preternatural matriarchal "Sight." And at this pivotal moment in her life, Andry knew it with a certainty she'd never before felt about anything. What she didn't yet know was the form it would take, its extent, and the final result.

What she did know was that it was more than just the Sight she vaguely recalled her bio-em singing about to her while she was being tucked away to sleep in her infant cradle. And what she would later learn as an adult was that her version of the Sight had come packaged with another gift buried deep within—a gift that she was certain could only have come from Amelie Stewart: the inner strength to control and command the Sight and what it revealed. That was, as yet, a key part of her currently unresolved conundrum, and within that second gift, of which she was still not fully aware, she would eventually find the answer to her needs, wants and desires both now and in the future with Rob.

She had never talked of this with her custodians, PerCust, group or nest mates. As an infant, she had been too young to verbalize what she was thinking. She had never talked about it even with her closest childhood friends, Rob and Frann. On the other hand, she'd often wondered at the feeling of power within her that had, in her mind, through Amelie Stewart also empowered Tripler and Clarke though not Jackson. Being the offspring of someone so famous as to be regarded as a Goddess would have had its comps, but also its draws. Anonymity hadn't been as difficult to maintain as she had later worried. Much of what was publicly known of the times surrounding her conception and birth had been swept away when NewAmerica's leaders remade and rewrote history. And what was left had had been made to fit into an age where all knowledge of one's bio-parents was supposed to be, by law, denied to offspring.

The result was that a few considered NewAmerica an anathema to God, and Andry, because of her bios' fame, had no interest becoming their scapegoat. To Andry, NewAmerica was simply what it was: a pragmatic reality of the times set against the legendary, greater-than-life Tripler, Clark, Stewart and Jackson backdrop, a New Age schizophrenia that everyone acknowledged, and was, if anything, continuing to insidiously add to. Public feelings of patriotism for NewAmerica still ran high—some would say amok—during national holidays, and Andry had no interest in becoming a symbol of the past, present or future. She longed to be simply who she was, and, whoever that was, to begin to fulfill the destiny that had suddenly begun to weigh about and upon her, a destiny that despite all that she had recently come to know, she also knew had barely begun to unfold.

Chapter 32

A spiritual awakening of a kind began within the populace when NewAmerica officially formed. Religions—redefined and accepted as a social clubs, run as businesses, with the typical business *accouterments* such as "store fronts," prescriptive "dues," the selling of club literature and merchandise, as well as publicity, advertising and marketing to gain brand recognition and garner new members—had been around long before recorded civilization. The earliest archeological evidence from the Mediterranean documented the existence of prehistoric, organized Mother Goddess cults, and the desire for individuals to establish a connection between themselves and a greater power is assumed to have long predated these cults. The desire to organize and businessify spirituality into religions was more recent. Although there had never existed any direct evidence, it had always been assumed that the search for a deeper meaning in life was synonymous with spirituality and religion, inevitably linking the two, an assumption felt unnecessary in contemporary NewAmerica, NewTerra and beyond. Rather, it was now widely acknowledged that in Brown's day, truly spiritual individuals were often not necessarily religious, and religious individuals were often not necessarily spiritual. Religious adherents typically *claimed* to be spiritual, though their religions were coming under increasing public scrutiny for inconsistencies in both their belief systems—some religions were frankly outrageous in nature—and in regard to their business practices—a growing number being outright criminal. During President Brown's administration, spirituality and religion rarely intersected, and when they did, social strife followed and yet another another new religion typically resulted.

Though the ancient Mother Goddess cults had completely disappeared, supplicants of the Mother Goddess continued to quietly worship and maintain her existence, first alongside whatever god (typically male) who was in vogue, and later, in the form of a mother figure associated with the practice of nature and environmental conservation. One religion in particular, Wicca, though it boasted few adherents prior to Brown's term, claimed to reunite spirituality and religion in just such a way. Until the Total Meltdown.

Clandestine Mother Goddess worshippers during the Meltdown left the various religions in droves to join like minded "green" individuals, increasingly in surreptitious

Wiccan covens that had, to everyone's surprise, existed scattered throughout the old United States of America for hundreds of years, the highly organized "Bible Belt" religions working constantly to "dam(n) the flood" and keep the movement strictly in check.

Coming "out of the closet" at last, Wiccans began publicly celebrating the Mother Goddess and her historical seasonal festivals, despite being proportionally vilified by the other religions, especially those that were rapidly losing membership. One tactic to curb the upstarts was to namecall Wiccans "witches." Despite this, Wicca became the new catholic (meaning universal) religion, accepting religious and non-religious spiritual individuals alike. Like so many other social changes of the time, it was a wholly "grass-roots" phenomenon with new covens springing up every day, mostly without an established business hierarchy. Wicca swept the fledgling NewAmerica and NewTerra like a perfect storm.

Andry knew all of this. At its heart, the Mother Goddess and her "Wiccan" re-manifestation were, in her mind, neither dark nor evil. Wicca was simply a new old way to express spirituality. At its core, it was about devotion so deep it could exert a subtle but profound influence over all things, especially humans, animals and plants—even non-living rocks and streams—and through that devotion an individual's destiny. It was about channeling Goddess' energy, always available without reservation to followers who knew its correct name and incantation, written, spoken or thought, to summon the energy from the nether into the current world. Its most fundamental difference from other religions, and the main reason it caught on so quickly in NewAmerica, was that it was *completely volitional*. One could join, leave and rejoin at any time without impunity. During the social maelstrom, some non-Wiccan NewAmericans, came to regard Wicca as a non-religion, to others anti-religious. The same people, by Andry's experience, also remained stubbornly ignorant of the very force which could afford them a much-needed alternative perspective on life.

One of Andry's friends from another mob who joined a different foray had introduced her to several enlightened Wiccans who immediately recognized in her an inner power, ancient and maternalistic. Within days, Andry became the *de facto* leader of their coven, absorbing and reciting the coven spells and rituals as if she already knew them, in the process—at least from the coven members' perspective—acquiring individual and increasing their collective spiritual power. She was, everyone said in a reverentially subdued tone, a "natural witch." The coven's size immediately began to increase, and under Andry's guidance, as it grew, the divide between spirituality and religion lessened even further.

Andry, in turn, dived deep into the occult, becoming increasingly interested in her purported ancient past while displaying ever more openly her desire for Rob on the sleeves of her white flowing Wiccan robes. To the coven's delight, she openly shared whatever she discovered with everyone, while fearlessly experimenting on herself, exploring ever further her relationship to Wicca and the Mother Goddess. In regard to Rob (now Draff to her). Andry's question seemed no longer "if," but how to invoke her growing power to resolve her current Draff conundrum. When she did figure it all out, according to all she'd learned, there would be draw—there was always draw—and the more she called upon her power, the greater that draw would likely be.

At the same time, coven members began murmuring that she, as their leader, was in need of a partner—a warlock or male witch—to help her focus her power. The question soon floating anxiously in the air was whether she would take one in order to wield her power to gain Draff's attention and affection. Something within her warned that if she wanted Draff, she would have to first pay the coven draw, locating and selecting a suitable warlock soon and decisively. In her mind, that moment presented when Remi Edward Alex

[Corsi-Mant] asked her join his adult foray, and be his FLIC.

Edward was a close, and by most foray member's reckoning, socially intimate friend of Billie, and like Billie, gay in interest, proclivity, and action. What only a select few knew was that he, like Andry, was the leader of a coven. Though small and largely male, it was a long-established coven held in high esteem by knowledgeable Wiccans. As the coven's outstanding warlock, he was handsome, prominent, available, and known to be actively searching for a female counterpart. Very available, at his coven's urging, though personally reluctant, given his innate sexual preference and the orthodox requirement that, in order to join their covens under a High Priestess and Principal Warlock, the two were required to join sexually. The moment he heard of Andry through Draff and Billie, Edward invited her to join his foray with the intent of eventually asking her to be his Wiccan counterpart. *If*, that is, she would acquiesce and joined his foray. *If* he was attractive to her. *If* she was willing to be his FLIC. *If* she could tolerate his being gay— she seemed to be attracted to both Draff and Billie and tolerate their being gay. And *if* she was—and he truly hoped she would turn out to be—Wiccan *and* willing to be his High Priestess. It was an incredibly long shot, but…

While Andry was enjoying the thought that her invite to join Edward's foray was the result of Draff and Billie's insistence, there was no question in Edward's mind about the felicitousness of their meeting and all living together. Each of the four was, at least to the casual eye, a perfect complement to the other. When Edward asked Andry to be his FLIC, she had, to Edward's initial disappointment hesitated, but to his later delight ended up nodding in the affirmative, and to his unbounded joy she grazed his palm in the secret, proscribed Wiccan gesture of welcome. By returning the gesture, each immediately knew the other was Wiccan and might be the much anticipated answer to his and her prayers. In the end, it all depended on how much each was willing to sacrifice in order to satisfy their carefully uncommunicated, innermost needs and desires.

Physical sex between the two would, of course, be essential, but the ritual joining didn't require love or affection—just mutual purpose and respect for each other during the performance. By doing this, the members of both covens understood their collective and individual spiritual powers would automatically increase. Remi, who had reluctantly confided in her his sexual predilection for males, was now outwardly, though not inwardly Remi to Andry, who was now outwardly, but would never be inwardly Simi to him. Together, he would elevate her spells into *uber*-spells, massively increasing her power to inveigle divine help from the Mother Goddess. Outwardly

Remi totally embodied the Athame, the long, black, ceremonial dagger, needed to complement Andry's shorter and more delicate white knife. She, in turn, would wrap him and the two covens within her powerfully augmented protection, using him as the spark for her spells and incantations. Simi half-frowned, half-smiled at the thought of the confident warlock and their seemingly inevitable physical union—their own unusual SweetSixteenSalsaSexcapade. The joining of a witch leader with her chosen warlock would elevate the two to High Priestess and Principal Warlock, but the process would be more discrete, viewed by and known only to the members of the two joining covens. *I wonder if Edward is thinking of our upcoming union*, Andry mused. *And if so, I wonder if it will be as himself making love with Billie rather than me.*

In fact, Edward wasn't thinking at all of making love to Billie. He was imagining himself wielding enormous power—with Simi's tacit assistance, of course—to spell or charm Billie into the kind of "real" relationship for which the two, he would make certain, were secretly yearning. Simi, for her part, was imagining herself wielding the requisite power—with Remi's tacit assistance, of course— to completely transform the wobbling nexus that Draff and Billie were hopelessly attempting build. It would then be up to her to gently nudge Draff into smelling her at the center of that nexus, she reassured herself nervously. It wasn't that long a shot really, but still…

Thinking solely of Draff, Simi could envision a later, only slightly less ostentatious but definitely more fulfilling event with him than his and Billie's outrageously famous SweetSixteenSalsaSextravaganza. She could accept, she assured herself, her physical joining with both men, Draff as lover and soul mate, and Remi as the needed match to ignite her innate power. She could feel behind her navel the raw power that her FLIC with Edward the Principal Warlock would conjure, forcing fate to stretch out its hand and forge her and Draff's destinies at last into one. Draff would have only to accept. Willingly, of course, and most of all knowingly, with open eyes, heart and spirit. "Open eyes, heart and spirit," she repeated aloud to herself as if attempting to justify that what she was going to do was solely for Draff, the ancients, the coven, and her own uncontainable desire for Draff Rob Brie [Septican-Smite]. But she would have to first accept Remi Edward Alex [Corsi-Mant] as her FLIC and Wiccan mate—pay the draw— in order to secure her and Draff's common destiny. Before her welcoming party at her new adult foray was over, Andry had formally met Edward and discretely but clearly indicated her resolve to serve as his High Priestess. *But that's all*, Simi reminded herself. *Just a FLIC and the door to my and Draff's future will finally open*, her mind echoed, *That's all. Right?*

Throughout that evening, Draff, oblivious to Andry and Edward's secret liaison, had nonetheless smelled an unfamiliar indifference in the air whenever he was near Simi and decided to give her space to resolve whatever it was that was bothering her. Simi, on the other hand, felt Draff was ignoring her—intentionally or unintentionally she couldn't tell, but hoped and prayed it was the latter. Billie watched Draff and Simi from a careful distance, like a hawk searching for a kill. To Simi, Billie seemed to be studying her every motion, every eye blink,, every wave of her hand, as if he were trying to read, she assumed, with Draff and her in such close proximity, her intentions. But it wasn't the cool intensity of Billie's stare that unnerved her so much as it was that she couldn't find a reason why it should.

The next evening at another location which she was careful to not disclosed to Draff, Billie or the other members of her new foray, Andry/Simi took Edward/Remi as her Principal Warlock, and he took her as his High Priestess, each in flesh but neither in heart.

It was a highly ritualistic ceremony—tepid yet sufficiently satisfying to the newly combined coven members, and bestial enough to temporarily satisfy Remi. It began at midnight and didn't finish until dawn.

Chapter 33

The ceremony began at the stroke of midnight. Simi, wearing a flowing white robe, was escorted into the torch-lit room by a black caped and hooded Remi. After walking hand-in-hand around the outside the circle of the fifty or so combined chanting coven members, Semi led Remi into the center and drew a sacred circle about them and the central alter with the point of a staff, holding Remi's surprisingly cold quivering hand in the other. After an appropriate pause, Simi took her place on the right side of the gold-draped altar while Remi took his on the opposite side.

Momentarily parting the folds of her robe, Semi's pearl white body glowed in the dimly flickering candlelight making her seem the Goddess incarnate. Remi shifted his weight, looked over at her and absent-mindedly fingered the black knife slung about his bare hip. Her other-worldly appearance thrust him from the present into a waking dream where he was walking, naked, hand-in-hand not with the Goddess Simi, but a naked and willing Billie.

Simi raised from the altar a gold-leafed earthen goblet

intricately carved with filigreed runic cursives, the incised cursives flashing like shooting stars in the flickering light. Holding it in both hands above her head and offering it to the unseen Mother Goddess above, she whispered the required incantation, slowly brought the cup back down to her lips and drank deeply. Finished, she carried the cup in both hands to the other side of the altar and, eyes cast down, offered it to Remi.

Remi, hands still shaking, accepted the cup which Simi envisioned offering not the timorous man facing her, but to an emboldened Draff. Raising the cup above his head, he whispered the remainder of the incantation, brought the cup to his lips, drank deeply, then suddenly cast the cup hard onto the floor. The cup shattered with a gun-like report into a thousand brilliant pieces and in the nebulous darkness about them, the coven members began the requisite chant.

This time, it was Simi, who, as if awaking from her dream, bent before Remi on one knee, then at his command, stood, turned and made a path for her chosen warlock to follow her to the front of the altar in the center of the two protective circles—one drawn by her, the other formed by the two covens together—about them. Facing the altar with Remi directly behind her, the black caped and hooded members watched as the figure behind her stretched out his arms, his cape hiding from direct view what was inevitably about to happen. As if on command, the outer circle drifted closer to bear witness to Simi and Remi's well planned and much better executed SweetSixteenSalsaSex FLIC.

Silence fell when Simi dropped her robe and Remi encircled their two bodies with his jet black cape. The crowd gasped as Simi thrust her white knife high above, Remi thrust his long black blade up beside hers, and Simi issued a wailing cry as Remi touch the tip of his blade to hers.

The pair, now one in everyone's mind, still holding high the touched tips of the white and black knives, were engulfed in a cone of brilliant white light issuing from above, illuminating the sea of black-robed figures huddling as close as humanly possible about their new High Priestess and Principal Warlock. This was the moment of their combined empowerment, and the crowd about them transformed into a black vortex of writhing, chanting bodies inseparable one from another.

Simi and Remi didn't notice. Their part in the ritual had been more than successful. The power they each sought, though for each's different personal reasons, was now complete. Remi, now Principal Warlock, had, if not by sexual inclination, then at least physically opened the door to his eventual conquest of Billie. Simi, now High Priestess, had, if not romantically, then at least physically continued her inward journey into adulthood and eventual pairing with

Draff while receiving at the same time, the sacred blessing of none other than the Mother Goddess herself.

Chapter 34

Two weeks later, Draff made an official announcement from the foray's shared master room: Slamming these last few weeks had been so successful, he had saved enough to pay for a *private* ARS by the best on the planet. Armed with plentiful self-interested advice from his many slamming clients and friends, Draff had booked the clinic and completed the necessary interviews and genotyping. He was ready to walk in next morning a skin-virgin and walk out with a fully working, though admittedly somewhat tender, simian tail.

The entire foray celebrated his continued ascent into adulthood. Billie smelled and looked unfazed. Andry smelled and looked stunned, then incredulous, then annoyed, aggravated and finally disgusted. *What is with Simi?* Draff wondered, raising his eyebrows at the staccato olfactory slaps he sensed coming from her, all seeming aimed directly at him. Why did he feel so hurt? More important, why should her reactions bother him so deeply, or at all for that matter?

Draff noticed Billie staring at Simi. *And what's with*

those two? he thought before his better judgment kicked in and he dismissed his conflicting thoughts, reburying himself in the tsunami of forearm-clasps, hugs and well-wishes.

Everything is going so well, he reflected happily.

Everything isn't quite coming together as I'd hoped, Simi reflected with concern.

Everything is going to hell, Billie reflected angrily.

President-Elect Mathias "Alexander the Great" Jackson learns on election eve that the current President has resigned with over a trillion dollars in petroleum securities, leaving the US leaderless and facing an economic crisis of unparalleled proportions. President Jackson, wrongly accused of manufacturing the crisis, turns to his two must trusted political aides, Adelphous Tripler and Shawn Clarke. Committed lovers, Tripler and Clarke must reluctantly separate to carry out a series of incredibly challenging tasks for their discredited leader that takes them around the globe. With murder and mayhem facing them every step of the way, will they manage to get back to each other alive?

Koski and Falk come up against what very well may prove to be their most complex and dangerous case yet: The Quantum Death Machine. Each faces mortal peril, while, at the same time, their smoldering relationship begins to heat up. The fifth in the seven-book Koski & Falk Series by A. G. Hayes.

Raymond Gaynor is the pen-name of the multi-awarded, reclusive writer. artist, photographer, videographer who, in his own words, "lives and breathes" San Francisco. He co-authored with William Maltese on the Tripler and Clarke gay political thriller, TOTAL MELTDOWN (Borgo/Wildside 2009) and with A. G. Hayes on the fifth Koski & Falk adventure, QUANTUM DEATH (Savant 2016). He is the author of numerous fiction and non-fiction works published under a number of different pseudonyms.

If you enjoyed *The Edge of Madness,* consider these other fine books from Aignos Publishing:

The Dark Side of Sunshine by Paul Guzzo
Cazadores de Libros Perdidos by German William Cabasssa Barber [Spanish]
The Desert and the City by Derek Bickerton
The Overnight Family Man by Paul Guzzo
There is No Cholera in Zimbabwe by Zachary M. Oliver
John Doe by Buz Sawyers
The Piano Tuner's Wife by Jean Yamasaki Toyama
An Aura of Greatness by Brendan P. Burns
Polonio Pass by Doc Krinberg
Iwana by Alvaro Leiva
University and King by Jeffrey Ryan Long
The Surreal Adventures of Dr. Mingus by Jesus Richard Felix Rodriguez
Letters by Buz Sawyers
In the Heart of the Country by Derek Bickerton
El Camino De Regreso by Maricruz Acuna [Spanish]
Prepositions by Jean Yamasaki Toyama
Deep Slumber of Dogs by Doc Krinberg
Saddam's Parrot by Jim Currie
Beneath Them by Natalie Roers
Chang the Magic Cat by A. G. Hayes
Illegal by E. M. Duesel
Island Wildlife: Exiles, Expats and Exotic Others by Robert Friedman
The Winter Spider by Doc Krinberg
The Princess in My Head by J. G. Matheny
Comic Crusaders by Richard Rose
I'll Remember by Clif Mc Crady
Critical Writing: Stories as Phenomena by Jamie Dela Cruz Ed.D

Coming Soon:
The City and the Desert by Derek Bickerton
'Til then Our Written Love Will Have to Do by Cheryl L. Woods

The Edge of Madness

…and these other fine books from our parent company Savant Books and Publications:

Essay, Essay, Essay by Yasuo Kobachi
Aloha from Coffee Island by Walter Miyanari
Footprints, Smiles and Little White Lies by Daniel S. Janik
The Illustrated Middle Earth by Daniel S. Janik
Last and Final Harvest by Daniel S. Janik
A Whale's Tale by Daniel S. Janik
Tropic of California by R. Page Kaufman
Tropic of California (the companion music CD) by R. Page Kaufman
The Village Curtain by Tony Tame
Dare to Love in Oz by William Maltese
The Interzone by Tatsuyuki Kobayashi
Today I Am a Man by Larry Rodness
The Bahrain Conspiracy by Bentley Gates
Called Home by Gloria Schumann
First Breath edited by Z. M. Oliver
The Jumper Chronicles by W. C. Peever
William Maltese's Flicker by William Maltese
My Unborn Child by Orest Stocco
Last Song of the Whales by Four Arrows
Perilous Panacea by Ronald Klueh
Falling but Fulfilled by Zachary M. Oliver
Mythical Voyage by Robin Ymer
Hello, Norma Jean by Sue Dolleris
Charlie No Face by David B. Seaburn
Number One Bestseller by Brian Morley
My Two Wives and Three Husbands by S. Stanley Gordon
In Dire Straits by Jim Currie
Wretched Land by Mila Komarnisky
Who's Killing All the Lawyers? by A. G. Hayes
Ammon's Horn by G. Amati
Wavelengths edited by Zachary M. Oliver
Communion by Jean Blasiar and Jonathan Marcantoni
The Oil Man by Leon Puissegur
Random Views of Asia from the Mid-Pacific by William E. Sharp

Raymond Gaynor

The Isla Vista Crucible by Reilly Ridgell
Blood Money by Scott Mastro
In the Himalayan Nights by Anoop Chandola
On My Behalf by Helen Doan
Chimney Bluffs by David B. Seaburn *The Loons* by Sue Dolleris
The Judas List by A. G. Hayes
Path of the Templar—Book 2 of The Jumper Chronicles by W. C. Peever
The Desperate Cycle by Tony Tame
Shutterbug by Buz Sawyer
Blessed are the Peacekeepers by Tom Donnelly and Mike Munger
Bellwether Messages edited by D. S. Janik
The Turtle Dances by Daniel S. Janik
The Lazarus Conspiracies by Richard Rose
Purple Haze by George B. Hudson
Imminent Danger by A. G. Hayes
Lullaby Moon (CD) by Malia Elliott of Leon & Malia
Volutions edited by Suzanne Langford
In the Eyes of the Son by Hans Brinckmann
The Hanging of Dr. Hanson by Bentley Gates
Flight of Destiny by Francis Powell
Elaine of Corbenic by Tima Z. Newman
Ballerina Birdies by Marina Yamamoto
More More Time by David B. Seabird
Crazy Like Me by Erin Lee
Cleopatra Unconquered by Helen R. Davis
Valedictory by Daniel Scott
The Chemical Factor by A. G. Hayes
Quantum Death by A. G. Hayes and Raymond Gaynor
Big Heaven by Charlotte Hebert
Captain Riddle's Treasure by GV Rama Rao
All Things Await by Seth Clabough
Tsunami Libido by Cate Burns
Finding Kate by A. G. Hayes
The Adventures of Purple Head, Buddha Monkey and... by Erik & Forest Bracht
In the Shadows of My Mind by Andrew Massie
The Gumshoe by Richard Rose
In Search of Somatic Therapy by Setsuko Tsuchiya

The Edge of Madness

Cereus by Z. Roux
The Solar Triangle by A. G. Hayes
Shadow and Light edited by Helen R. Davis
A Real Daughter by Lynne McKelvey
StoryTeller by Nicholas Bylotas
Bo Henry at Three Forks by Daniel Bradford
Kindred edited by Gary "Doc" Krinberg
Cleopatra Victorious by Helen R. Davis
Navel of the Sea by Elizabeth McKague
Entwined edited by Gary "Doc" Krinberg
Truth and Tell Travel the Solar System by Helen R. Davis
The COMPLETE Koski & Falk by A. G. Hayes
Leon & Malia's ISLAND MUSIC: Classic Songs from the Hawaiian Islands
Clean Water, Common Ground (DVD) by Daniel S. Janik/Mary Tuti Baker

Coming Soon
Honeymoon Forever: Find Love, Keep Love by R. Page Kaufman
Aloha La'a Kea (Sacred Light of Love) edited by Uhene
Hawaii Kid's Music Vol I & II (music CD) by Leon and Malia

Savant Books and Publications
www.savantbooksandpublications.com